BREAKING BREAD

BOOK 5: THE RUNESPELL SERIES

SARAH BUHRMAN

Black Rose Writing | Texas

ISBN: 978-1-68513-400-6
PUBLISHED BY BLACK ROSE WRITING
www.blackrosewriting.com

Printed in the United States of America
Suggested Retail Price (SRP) $19.95

Breaking Bread is printed in Adobe Caslon Pro

*As a planet-friendly publisher, Black Rose Writing does its best to eliminate unnecessary waste to reduce paper usage and energy costs, while never compromising the reading experience. As a result, the final word count vs. page count may not meet common expectations.

Thank you to E. Christopher Clark who beta read
and inspired me to get it done.

Thank you to Cat Rambo who decided I actually knew
what I was doing enough to teach some classes.

Thank you to the state of Michigan, which has renewed my faith
in humanity and nature. I'm so glad to have moved here.

BREAKING BREAD

CHAPTER 1

I stared up at the skyscraper, wondering what awaited me here in this strange, new place. I really didn't want to be in Sacramento, but I couldn't continue to sulk in my house in Indiana forever.

I sighed as Ella and Maria jostled me rushing toward the hotel. I hurried to join them at the crosswalk before the light changed. When I held out my hands to them, Maria hesitated before slipping hers into mine. Ella just ignored me.

I sighed again. Tweens.

At least, I hoped it was just that. If it wasn't, then the girls were still upset about what had happened on the cruise.

I clamped down hard on that thought. That thought would lead to memories, and memories would lead to retraumatizing. I had stuff to do. I couldn't spend our vacation crying in a corner of the hotel room.

Entering the hotel, we all stopped at the sight of the lobby. A huge chandelier, hung with hundreds of crystals, hovered over a marble floor.

In the center, a stone wall towered over all our heads. Water gushed down, rippling over the stone's natural imperfections. The small pool at the bottom gurgled pleasantly, while a handful of small koi circled around.

The smell of flowers and expensive perfumes tickled my nose, contrasting with the tang of pollution that permeated the California coastal cities. The low murmur of people in conversation washed over me. Two men in suits strode past, neatly moving around us without even glancing our way.

I moved over to the long counter nestled against the wall. Several people in uniforms bustled around behind it, looking busy. I stepped up to one of the computers peeking over the edge of the counter. The young woman working on the machine clicked and tapped for several more seconds before looking up with a customer-service smile.

"How may I help you?"

I cleared my throat. "We have a reservation. I'm here for the conference on herbalism."

The woman turned her attention to the computer, clicking as rapidly as she fired questions at me. I signed the agreement as she slid a folded paper with two keycards across the counter. "Enjoy your stay."

I nodded and crossed back over the marbled lobby to the front door. Joseph grinned at me over the luggage cart he was pushing through the electric double doors.

"This place is fancy!" he said. "I wonder what the mini bar holds."

I scowled at him. "More debt than a student loan, is my guess. Let's get settled, then we can explore the city."

I turned to the girls who were still ogling the fountain and chandelier. "You figure out where the elevator is yet?" Maria nodded while Ella shrugged. I sighed. "Well, lead the way."

The three-bedroom suite was just as mind-boggling as the lobby, with a crystal studded accent wall greeting us at the door. We claimed our beds and unpacked quickly, then I dragged the kids away from the satellite cable TV and back to the rental car.

We found ourselves back on the highway heading north out of the city. I had heard wine country was this way, and I wanted to see some of it.

Joseph kept up a steady conversation of the goings on in the Indianapolis witchy community, and the girls alternately oohed and aahed, and rolled their eyes at my comments about the scenery.

Joseph and I were arguing about whether I had taken a wrong turn when we came upon a large group of people milling around the gated entrance to a large industrial building. The large, hyperboloid cement structures nearby labelled the building as a nuclear power plant, and the signs held by many of the people said things like "Use your cranium, not uranium" and "Hell no, we won't glow."

I exchanged a glance with Joseph. "You may be right," I admitted. "It might have been a wrong turn."

He snorted, running his hand over his thinning blond hair. "You think?"

I glared at him. "Just for that, I'm stopping to ask directions." I pulled up close to the back edge of the protest group and rolled down the window.

A woman about 10 years older than me ran her eyes over our car and landed on each of our faces. Her dark hair was pulled back into a function-over-form ponytail, and her weathered skin spoke of a life of outdoorsy-ness. She was dressed in worn but clean jeans and a cotton button-down with sturdy boots on her feet. It was the gleaming silver star at her throat that caught my eye, though.

She approached the car with a wary but open expression.

"Blessed be," I said awkwardly. I wasn't usually so forward with the Pagan jargon, but I figured her being more friendly wouldn't hurt.

She blinked as if surprised, then offered a reserved smile. "Merry meet, fellow travelers. What can I do for you?"

I offered her a smile of my own. "We seem to have taken an unexpected turn. What's going on here?"

The woman jutted her chin towards the building. "Ongoing safety concerns with the company. We want them to fix it or shut down. They don't want to spend the money."

I nodded. "Are they listening?"

The woman shrugged. "A bit. We have a meeting of sorts with the big wigs tomorrow night. It could be the breakthrough we've been hoping for."

I nodded. "To be a fly on the wall for that..."

She shrugged. "You're welcome to attend. Anyone with an opinion or support for either side is invited." She smiled wryly. "Besides, it's catered, so we need some people who aren't so tense that they can't eat."

I quickly calculated the seminar schedule and my own interest in the topic, then raised a questioning brow at Joseph. "You wanna?"

Joseph grinned. "I'm all for a cause. You know that." He shifted his attention to the woman. "Count us in."

The woman nodded. "I'm Isabel Johansson, the lead cat-herder for this rabble." She dug a card out of her pocket. "The location and times are all on the website, here, and you can email me with any questions."

I gave the woman our names, glancing at the card before handing it to Joseph. "I only have one question right now. Where's the Kingsford Vineyard?"

Isabel grinned. "Back down the road, take a left, first right. There's a sign, but it's kinda low and might be hidden in the grass if they haven't mown recently." She patted the door in a friendly gesture. "Try the chicken parm; it is fabulous. And I hope to see you tomorrow."

I waved as we pulled slowly away from the crowd. "Well, that was pleasant."

"And we get a free supper," Joseph added. "All around, it should be a great night."

I grinned, but the dread bubbled in my stomach. "Should be" almost never seemed to actually be these days.

CHAPTER 2

I heaved a sigh as we approached the conference room. This was either going to be a very nice time or a very bad time, and I was getting anxious because I didn't know which it would be. The feeling of dread had poked at me throughout the day, making me a little more tense and jumpy than I'd hoped for during this so-called vacation.

Joseph was a full step ahead of me, eager to dive in. But then, he enjoyed meeting new people and talking about topics that caused tension.

"We don't even know that much about these safety issues." I found myself repeating the same complaints I'd had all day. I knew it was ridiculous, and I was projecting my own issues onto the situation. I just couldn't seem to stop myself. It didn't help that I wasn't sure if I wanted Joseph to reassure me or validate my fears.

"If you didn't want to come, you could have stayed in with the girls instead of hiring that sitter," Joseph pointed out.

I shrugged, not willing to talk about the pressure I felt almost daily about being alone and a parent. I was beginning to notice thoughts that told me if I did anything for myself, I was a horrible parent and deserved to have the girls taken away.

I quickly steered my thoughts away from that emotional spiral. Ever since my mother had called CPS on me, I'd been circling the drain with that negative thinking. I knew it was just the anxiety talking.

My therapist, Dr Walters, said I was experiencing a kind of mild trauma-induced depression. She said the shock of my mom turning on me like that was affecting how safe I felt in the world as a whole.

I figured it was nothing compared to the rest of what I'd gone through, but that wasn't something I could drop on my therapist, even if I wanted to.

"Come on, Nicola," Joseph said cheerfully. "This will be a nice, intellectual evening of debate controlled by too much formality."

I reluctantly smiled at the ridiculous truth in his words. "Fine, let's go play with the rich and powerful, and those who would oppose them."

The murmur of dozens of conversations hit me like a wall as the doors opened. I tried not to flinch, but Joseph shot me a look that said he'd noticed. Instead of responding, I focused on the roomful of people in front of us. The lines had been drawn and the uniforms for each side were subtle but distinct.

About half wore some variation of suit, pantsuit or cocktail dress. The fabrics were fine, and the cut was tailored. The other half was more casually outfitted, wearing slacks and nice jeans with a business casual top.

One older man wore cowboy boots, a western snap-front shirt, a bolo, and carried a felt cowboy hat. He was facing down a woman in a business suit who spoke with her hands moving in large gestures. At her side, a younger man stood looking uncomfortable in a suit that bordered on being a tuxedo.

I shook my head and scanned the room. I wasn't even sure what I was looking for. I just figured I'd know it when I saw it. Instead, I spotted the buffet table. Shrugging, I made a beeline for it, picking up a small paper plate as I scanned the offerings.

I'd managed to snag some meats, cheeses, and a small mountain of fruits when Isabel appeared beside me with a man about her own age hovering next to her. His lean tanned face seemed locked in a sullen expression.

"You made it." She waved a hand at the man. "This is Leon, my right hand."

I nodded a greeting around a mouthful of melon, swallowing it quickly instead of savoring the fruit. "So how are the talks going?"

The man's face darkened as Isabel answered. "Not as well as we'd hoped, but not as poorly as we feared."

I blinked at them for a moment, pulling at the energy around them so I could see their emotions. After a slight resistance that I had no time to question, the second sight burst into my perception.

I frowned for a moment as the world went grayscale. The sounds around me muted and time seemed to stretch out. I felt like I was spinning around, the vertigo catching me off guard.

"-not willing to spend the money for equipment, even though it would save them in the long run."

I shook myself and concentrated on her words. "It isn't unusual for a corporation to prioritize quarterly gains," I murmured. "It's difficult to get these businesses to look ahead more than a couple months, even if it keeps the company growing and functional, long term."

Isabel nodded. "You want to help me explain that to the CFO?"

I quirked a smile. "Oh, sure. Sounds like a great time."

We both chuckled and I shook my head wryly. "Want to? Nope. But I will anyways."

The older woman gave me a grateful smile and led Leon and me over to a man in a basic gray suit. The CFO's hair was more salt than pepper, and he stood alone, watching the other attendees with an unreadable expression.

I checked his emotional energy, grateful that there was no pop of perception change and that the color stayed in the world around me this time. His energy, however, was a muted yellow-green, sour and bitter.

I instantly felt put off by the man, but, after glancing at Isabel, I pasted on a pleasant expression and prepared to engage him in deep debate.

"Mr. Dean Lytle? This is my associate, Leon Arenas, and a friend of our cause, Nicole...?" Isabel's face fell in a horrified expression.

I smiled understandingly at her. "Nicola Crandall, entrepreneur." I felt weird saying that, but it seemed appropriate to add something to my name.

Mr. Lytle looked down his nose at me, despite being only an inch or so taller. "Have you come to convince me to abandon our bottom line as well?"

I smirked. "You and I both know that won't happen. Your company is legally incorporated, right? All the legal implications and associated rulings put your bottom line firmly in the spot of most important thing. The question is, as a company, are you willing to go down after one or two more really profitable quarters? Or does the company have a goal of continuing long-term?" I popped a large chunk of melon into my mouth and raised my brows at him.

"Touché," he murmured. "Profit and sustainable business seldom go hand in hand, something many people don't realize."

I shrugged. "Probably more people than you think. We just don't understand why businesses would choose to go under. As individuals, we think of a business as something to start and carry on for years, even decades. The idea of a quick burning business seems... illogical."

Mr. Lytle tugged at one sleeve of his jacket. "That's the problem with laymen trying to influence corporate decision-making. It's a complete lack of understanding how the game is played at that level."

I cocked my head to the side. "That may have something to do with the fact that corporations grew out of a legal cooperative that was, by its nature, meant to be temporary."

Leon appeared at my side with two plates of cake, offering one to each of us. I exchanged my now-empty plate for his offered one with a grateful smile.

Crunching down on the walnuts in the spice cake, I listened to Mr. Lytle talk about the pros of incorporation. The cake was really good, and I spared a sympathetic thought for Joseph. He hated walnuts and wouldn't eat anything with them in it.

"I think the big concern," I said, swallowing the last bite of cake, "is that because no one is held legally responsible for the corporation as a whole, there is a perception that also no one feels morally responsible for the company's decisions, even as those decisions are being made by people. It comes across as the worst of mob mentality with an unhealthy smattering of dissociation from one's own actions, simply because those actions are a part of a larger whole."

Mr. Lytle cleared his throat, pausing to take a drink and set down his empty plate. "And how would you solve the problem, Ms. Crandall? The public considers any admission of moral responsibility to be an admission of legal guilt, and the legal system isn't much more discriminating on that." He cleared his throat again, tugging at his collar and tie.

I tried not to frown at him, though his actions were distracting. I swallowed a psychosomatic tickle in my own throat. "That is something I am, admittedly, not sure of. At least not for the end result. I think a group of legal and corporate representatives need to hash that out."

I cleared my throat. I realized it was extremely sore. I wondered if I'd strained my voice talking to Mr. Lytle, though that seemed unlikely.

Mr. Lytle began coughing. He clutched at his throat and his unreadable, snotty expression turned into fear.

"Help him!" a woman's voice called out. "He can't breathe!"

I turned to find a woman bent over her partner. He flailed on the ground, gasping. Isabel and Leon rushed over to help. Several other people began coughing loudly, and two more collapsed on the floor.

The murmur of conversation changed to the higher pitch of panic as more of the crowd called out for help.

After a quick examination of the man and a nearby woman who had passed out, as well as a few questions for several people, Isabel and Leon whispered urgently back and forth. Finally, Isabel nodded and pulled out her phone. Leon stood and ran out the door.

I dropped down next to Isabel and helped her loosen the man's tie. "What is it?"

Isabel's gaze jumped to my face for a moment. She tugged the tie off the man's throat before responding. "It looks like paraquat poisoning. We've called 9-1-1, but-" She bit her lip.

I swallowed. "That bad, huh? How is it treated?"

"Fuller's earth," she muttered. "Leon has a few bags in his truck. He does landscaping."

I nodded, trying not to think about how tight my own throat felt. Staying calm was important in an emergency, and I'd had plenty of opportunity to practice that. "So we all eat dirt until the medics get here?"

Isabel nodded, her eyes jerking to the door as Leon reappeared, a large white, plastic-weave bag on his shoulder. I blinked at the suddenly bright flicker of light off of something shiny on the side of the bag. The flicker perfectly coincided with the man's hand flailing toward my nose.

Isabel stood. "Everyone, please. We seem to have a serious situation. Many of us are experiencing symptoms of what we think might be paraquat ingestion. If you feel pain or tightness in your throat, you may be affected. The best thing you can do for that is to ingest Fuller's earth. Thankfully, we have some here. Please, try to stay calm. Emergency responders are on their way."

I watched Leon dump a fine, light brown powder into the pitchers of water and iced tea on the buffet. I hurried over to help stir it in. Meanwhile, Isabel led the anxious people still standing over to us and began pouring glasses of thin mud for people.

I accepted a cup and downed it, then helped take glasses over to those who had dropped to the ground from their symptoms. It was heartbreaking to watch people try to drink the muddy slurry with throats swollen so much they could hardly breathe. It seemed forever before the sirens sounded.

I kept moving around, taking glasses of muddy water to people. Finally, someone plucked the cup out of my hand.

"Miss? You need to come with me."

The young man had a gentle but firm voice, but his words made no sense. I blinked at him in confusion.

He pulled at my arm, drawing me toward the ambulance. "You need to stop moving around so much. You've been poisoned."

CHAPTER 3

Darkness kept swallowing my vision. There wasn't much to see – the ceiling of the ambulance, locking cabinets and cubby-holes along the sides. Every now and then, the nice young man's face appeared.

Suddenly, the scene changed. I was looking up at a woman with a concerned expression. The ceiling was no longer the smooth metal of the ambulance. It was rapidly moving, speckled white drop-ceiling tiles instead.

There seemed to be a lot of movement around me. People shouted out orders while others ran around and between them. The hollow thunk of plastic hitting plastic sounded out and I felt the jarring of an impact roll through my body.

The ceiling tiles stopped moving above me. A PA system emitted a loud sound that was supposed to be somewhat pleasant, but it was just another thing grabbing at my attention. I couldn't even make out the words that followed.

I focused on my breaths, trying to ignore the overwhelming sensory jumble around me. People grabbed my limbs, moving my arms and legs, or shifting my whole body.

I lost track of what was being done to me. The white of the ceiling tiles faded to darkness before returning. Over and over again.

A single word pierced my brain, cutting through the muted roar of the busy hospital: "Coma."

Suddenly, I heard it over and over, maybe a dozen times. I felt the warm pressure of magic and I recognized, somewhere in the back of my mind, what message I was being sent.

The darkness crept back over my eyes. I could feel a finality in it. Taking a deep breath, I wrestled with the confusion for control of my mind and will.

Finally, momentarily, I won. And I stepped into the astral plane.

*****

I floated for a long time, moving through the familiar surreal landscape. I couldn't tell you why I'd gone into the astral instead of just falling unconscious like a normal person. Except I wasn't normal. I was a quest hero. And a thoroughly broken one, at that.

I thought back to my induction years ago. Mercy had been the one who told me about the quest. The Valkyrie had technically given me a choice, but, like so many quest heroes before me, I'd felt that pursuing the Runespells was the only right choice, and thus the only real choice.

I'd regretted it ever since. Starting with Keith's death.

Catherine's death had been more recent, followed up by the unnecessary addition of my mother calling CPS on me. Just because a sea goddess and her little old kraken scared everyone.

That betrayal had nearly undone me. I'd given the girls some time, then brought them home with me. We hadn't seen much of my mother since. I was afraid she would take any innocent thing out of context to hurt me again. I was afraid she would hurt the girls the way she'd hurt me.

I passed the fields where the air swimmers played. The long grasses flowed in pink-colored breezes like ocean waves.

I shuddered at the reminder of my second drowning experience, which reminded me of my first one, too. It seemed like I was getting over each trauma only to be retraumatized. With bonus material.

The view also brought back memories of the original quest, when I'd just been trying to help Muriel. Instead, I had been chased by demons, hijacked by Satan, saved by Valkyries, and recruited by Odin. Along the way, I'd been hunted by Bob, arrested, overwhelmed by a memory bomb, shot, kicked around, and nearly blown up.

I huffed a wry laugh thinking about it. The good ol' days, when things had been relatively simple and straight-forward.

The fields gave way to forests, which gave way to a rocky beach. I floated over the water, staring into its depths. I used to love the water. Now it brought only painful memories.

I thought about the last few years. I found it odd how the physical aspect of the abuse I'd endured with Zaro barely crossed my mind. It had been humiliating, at first, but it seemed to be something I could deal with. That's what Dr. Walters said. She also said it was normal.

I nearly laughed aloud at that. Me? Normal?

The way he'd stolen my freedom to feel my real feelings, the way he'd used that to manipulate and control me – that was what stole my breath away even now. That was what froze me with fear. That was what brought tears to my eyes.

And that had been what originally brought out the full berserker, and what had suppressed it when I tried to learn to control it. The hard-won lesson had been learned during the manhunt on the Appalachian Trail.

Well, it had started as a vacation that turned into a manhunt, which had turned into a confrontation with Bob, Fenrir and Hel. Typical time off for me. Sure, I'd taken out Bob for good that time, but damned if it hadn't cost me a large chunk of both my soul and my sanity.

At least I'd gotten to resolve some of my previous issues along the way. Well, as much as I'd resolved anything. I mean, it kept popping up at weird and inconvenient times. I was beginning to think Dr. Walters was right. Recovery was a journey not a destination.

I spun in a horizontal roll as I floated over the water. Without a destination in mind, I was just drifting through the astral plane at random. It was funny how my escapism and addiction to the astral plane had somehow translated into the safest vacation I'd ever taken.

I mean, the hike along the Appalachian Trail had been a bust as vacations go. The cruise to Alaska had ended with a Titanic-style sinking of the ship, a confrontation with the terrifying goddess of the seas, and recovery on an island with way more politics and cultural conflict than should have been possible with such a small, unassuming village.

Both situations had resulted in deaths, and I still carried the guilt for them. I couldn't even work through them with my therapist. She would be obligated to report outright murder, even given the complex situations both of them had been.

But I was certainly paying for them either way. The second one had been witnessed by my mother and my kids. They didn't get the context, and they all blamed me for the fear and confusion because of it. I sighed. If only someone had listened to me when I told them all to leave. But nope. Everyone thought they knew best, and no one seemed to trust me.

I shook my head. Being bitter over that was a well-worn path that I didn't need to go down. Not here in the astral, where stray thoughts and strong emotions had very real effects.

I straightened up from my reclined pose and glanced around, suddenly wary of tricksters and shades. The first would be drawn to my chaotic moods and thoughts. The second would want to feed on me if I got too deep in my negative feelings. Relaxing, but not healthy. That's how the astral plane worked.

No astral creatures were hovering nearby, though. I sighed in relief. Since I was stuck in the astral for a while, I didn't need to be put in either of those situations. They tended to spiral beyond control really easily.

Technically, the astral plane was only one of several options of where I could go, but it was also the most neutral and relatively safe.

I could go to dream space and check out people's dreams. The risk there was of being sucked into and trapped by those dreams. There, the dreamer had control, and that control was emotional and subconscious, leading to dangerous or embarrassing situations more often than not.

The Akashic Library was handy, but without a goal in mind, it would just feed me random information....

I stopped abruptly. Information. Like what could have caused this coma. Was it the paraquat poisoning? It could have been, but then why were the ER doctors acting like there was something unusual going on?

I thought about the number of people who had come in. Sure, it had likely been overwhelming, but ERs dealt with stuff like that often enough. Bus accidents and such would bring in lots of patients, too. They were capable of dealing with a lot of similar patients all at the same time, particularly in such a large city. But the doctors and nurses had been... overwhelmed. And I wanted to know why.

With nothing else to do than to investigate my own poisoning, I focused my will and stepped across to the Akashic Library.

CHAPTER 4

The dry, dusty-mold scent of library stacks hit me first. I didn't usually lean into the library aspect of the Akashic records so much, but this time I was looking for hard research. That brought forth memories of a thousand movie scenes of people sitting, surrounded by books, with a single lamp on the table in front of them.

My hip bumped into the table full of books next to me. I eyed the hard-looking chair and then smiled. After a few seconds, the chair was gone. An extra-wide, overstuffed chaise stretched out alongside the table of books. Another second passed and then a plate of snacks appeared on the table within reach of the chaise.

I curled up on the chaise and picked up a book simply labeled "Poisons." I flipped to the table of contents and closed my eyes briefly, letting my energy stabilize before gently pushing toward the book with my request.

Two bookmarks appeared within the pages of the book, and I flipped to the first of them. The chapter was titled paraquat salts. I settled in to read up on the herbicide.

I nodded to myself while reading up on uses and background, though the history of its use in industry-related suicides was new information. Since it was used in landscaping so much, it was often readily available around corporate buildings.

The treatment included information about fuller's earth, which put aside the slight doubts I'd had about Isabel and Leon's treatment of the victims. The rest of the information on treatment was dismal at best.

There were simply no really effective treatments for the toxicity once it entered one's system. The only thing doctors could do is treat the specific symptoms that popped up and hope the damage was minimal and not permanent.

I tore my gaze away from the text, trying to control my emotions. Sure, I had good reason to feel sorry for myself, but it still wouldn't help. There was no help. "I'd do almost as well having some ancient shaman shaking rattles over my body to chase away the evil toxic spirits."

I shook my head at the bitter thought.

"That's not fair."

I looked up at the voice. It was a woman who looked and sounded a lot like me.

This had happened before in the Library. People who talked things out often found that the Library provided a kind of reflection of the person themselves to act as a soundboard.

I liked to talk things out because it slowed down my jumpy, sometimes erratic flow of thought.

The reflection spoke again. "You've known people who do spiritual healing. You've done it yourself, in fact. The process is a little more nuanced than rattles and spirits."

I nodded, talking through the process. "It usually involves entering the body in an astral-projected form. You find energetic imbalances and kinda tweak them back closer in harmony. Then the body can better heal itself."

The reflection leaned forward encouragingly. "Is it hard?"

I shook my head. "It can be very draining on the practitioner, though that can be balanced out by a number of things. Ironically, working on oneself seems to be the least draining..."

I sat up straight, smacking my hand against my own forehead. "Nicola, sometimes you miss the forest for the trees!"

"You remembered...?"

I leaned on the armrest of the chair. "I could do healing on myself. Sure it might not do much, but at least I'd feel like I was doing something."

The reflection nodded. "Feeling productive is important. It helps you stay positive, and that's good for recovery."

I pulled the book back onto my lap.

"What are you doing now?" the reflection asked.

"Looking up symptoms," I muttered. "If I know what to look for and where, I can visualize things more clearly. I just need to find out what's being affected."

I flipped the pages, scanning through the text. "Here we go. Paraquat in the US is sold with safeguard agents added, including something to cause vomiting. That explains why everyone started gagging and choking."

I turned the page. "Damages the linings of the mouth and digestive tract. Ugh! Toxic effects primarily target lungs, liver and kidneys. Okay, that's helpful. Can result in heart failure, kidney failure, liver failure, and lung scarring." I looked up at the reflection. "Damn."

I flipped to the next page. "Hm, no indication of coma. Odd." I closed the book with a thud and stretched. "Well, that gives me something to start with, at least."

I floated out of the chaise, waving to the reflection as she faded out of sight. "Time to get to work." I stepped back into the astral plane, focusing on the part of the world that reflected where my body was. I found myself on a small island surrounded by a bog. My feet hovered above the swampy ground, and I peered through trees and grasses growing in a tangle of life and rot.

Birds and insects moved amongst the plant life, often stopping to prune dead leaves, pull off dying mosses, or remove odd, slug-like things from boughs. Each tree was a patient in the hospital.

I looked up at the pacific yew hovering behind me. The tree seemed healthy, though the branches drooped a little too much. Several of the spiney leaves had fallen into the water around the tiny plot of dry land where the trunk entered the ground.

I studied the base of the trunk for a moment, floating in a circle around the tree. I wasn't sure what I was looking for, only that it would lead me into the tree. I could feel the kinship with the arching branches and drooping twigs. It was my own body.

Finally, I spotted the little burrow under the fallen needles. It seemed to lead directly to the roots. I reached for it, letting my astral body stretch and shrink into a form that would fit through the small tunnel.

The space was dark, filled with the scent of wet dirt and decaying plant life. It was a green scent, and the energy was a not-quite-healthy shade of lime green. I could feel it covering my limbs with a vaguely slimy coat.

I pushed with my will in an attempt to shed the film before I entered my body. Most of it sloughed off. Then I passed through a kind of barrier.

I recognized it as my personal shielding, but it took me by surprise. I'd entered my body in astral form before, though I'd been conscious. The difference between entering as an internal dive and doing it as if the body was that of another person was astonishing.

I'd never had to encounter my own shields before, and I stopped to examine them. Compared to others, they were pretty standard, buffering external energy rather than fully blocking it.

Overall, I had to admit they were good shields. I didn't maintain them as often as many others did, so I let a small sense of pride wash over me.

After my moment of indulgence, I continued on into the bloodstream. The superhighway of cellular nutrition and waste disposal was usually the easiest way to get through a body. Organs tended to throw off direction and speed, in my experience. I figured it had something to do with the energy lines moving throughout.

It took only a moment for me to find the liver. The great detoxifier of mammals, the smooth, dark red triangle pulsed with the blood that filtered through it every second of every day. I could feel the inherent richness of the flesh, but what I was looking for would be new toxins. So I dug a little deeper.

I found it in the quadrate lobe between the gall bladder and the ligament that divided the liver into two distinct parts. The area pulsed more angrily, and the energy there was more of a bright red with sickly, yellow-brown spots so dark they looked black.

The yellow-brown blackness seemed to seep into the surrounding tissue, growing like an ink stain. I could see how the toxicity was affecting the energy and health of the tissues.

I reached out to touch it and drew back at the feeling of corruption that flowed up my arm. This was going to be harder than I'd thought. I took a deep breath.

CHAPTER 5

I considered the problem for a moment. Adding energy to the affected spot could increase the toxin's effects. It was best to just consider the already affected area as lost.

I heaved a sigh. "At least the liver can regenerate," I told myself aloud. The thought wasn't as comforting as I'd hoped.

I turned my attention to the area around the spot. Looking closer, I could see the battle raging on a cellular and energetic level. The monstrous toxin was barely held back by the smaller but more numerous filtration and detoxification cells.

I nodded, deciding on my course of action. I focused my will and began producing a general support energy. It was pretty standard in healing – just a bit of extra oomph to help out the systems already in place for repairing damage to the body.

The golden energy flowed around my astral arms and gathered at my hands. I traced my fingers around the cells that were holding the line, then fed the energy to them.

There was an immediate effect, with the liver cells surging up to hold back the toxic advancement. It looked as though the cells had a combination of beefing up and reinforcements, with extra defenses.

I just hoped that the boost would be enough to keep the toxins in check until they could be processed by the liver, and without so much damage to the organ that it stopped working. I watched long enough to make sure that the boost wasn't a quickly fading one before I moved on.

Shifting back into the circulatory system, I headed for the kidneys. They were the next most likely to fail and, while dialysis was an option, I didn't relish the thought of being locked into a schedule of procedures like that.

I found the kidneys and quickly glanced them over. The left seemed to be struggling more, so I went into it first. A quick scan showed that there was an overall effect of the toxin, rather than a single, concentrated location.

I got to work, using the golden energy to support the renal cells, a rich green to heal the damage, and a web of energy that looked like white cheesecloth to help purify the toxins. It took quite a while to adequately visualize and apply each bit of energy. Plus, I had to layer them over and over to ensure the effects would last.

I could feel the strain of the prolonged concentration. From a biological perspective, I was just technically thinking thoughts with feeling, but the result was a pervasive fatigue. I finished with the one organ and moved on to its twin, repeating the whole process. At some point during my work, I began to lose focus.

My energy started to sputter and leech away, and I found myself drifting away from the kidney. I had to reorient myself several times before I could finish. I was nearly done when I started drifting off again.

The energy faded from around my hands and my perspective began to rotate as I floated, untethered. I didn't notice the lack of energy when I reached out to run my astral fingers through the tainted organ tissue.

Cold, paralyzing shock immediately crawled up my hand to my arm. I stared in disbelief as my astral limb turned black and hard before my eyes.

"Oh gods!" My mind raced through ideas of how to combat this corruption. Then my other hand went numb.

I looked at it and saw that I'd drifted into a toxin pocket while distracted. That settled it. I gasped a breath, pulled my will together with an almost physical feeling to the effort, and stepped back into the astral plane proper.

After a moment of reorienting myself, I focused my energy on my hands, willing the golden light to push back the black corruption. It took a disturbingly long time for the effect to appear, but it did in the end.

I shook out my stiff fingers and flexed them several times. Relief flooded through me that I'd been able to fix them at all, but disappointment reared up at the knowledge that I no longer had the energy to maintain focus.

"Geez, Nicola," I muttered to myself. "Cut you some slack. You don't even know how long you were working on that shit. I mean, it felt like forever..." I sighed. "Maybe I should take a break."

I immediately considered my options. I would need a place where it was relatively safe to lose all concentration. Most creatures who spent time in the astral had a pocket of their own, a kind of den of controlled reality.

Mortals, however, just went back to their bodies. I didn't have that option. Not while comatose. At least not so long as I wanted to be able to come back here. For now, it was this or complete loss of consciousness, even on a soul level.

"What I need is crash space," I grumbled. "Hey, can I sleep on your astral couch? At what price to my spirit?" I barked a laugh.

"Astral couch is yours, no cost," a croaking voice said behind me.

Another almost identical voice joined the first. "Our world, a haven, for what you've lost."

The smile was on my face before I turned to face the ravens. "Huginn! Muninn! My heroes!"

"You need to rest," Huginn croaked.

Muninn bobbed his head. "You drain yourself."

I nodded reluctantly. "I know, I know. I overextended myself." I stretched my limbs. I knew I looked ridiculous doing so while floating in mid-air. "Can you lead the way?"

The ravens exchanged a look. "Yes, but no."

"We shouldn't be here."

"So we cannot lead you from here."

"But we can show the path."

I nodded. The ravens could break the rule that kept gods out of the astral plane, but they didn't want the other gods to know that. It would make their lives and jobs... complicated. I was in on their secret, and I respected their desire to keep it.

"Is it the bifrost then?" I asked, looking over at the silver-blue ribbon that cut through the sky of the astral plane. "How do I travel on it?"

"Wait for the feel..."

"...of your destination."

"Then get off there," they finished together.

I grinned. "Sounds about right. Where am I going, exactly, and what is the 'feel' of that place?"

The ravens exchanged a look.

"It feels like Odin," they said. "You go to Valhalla."

Huginn hopped forward. "But a warning."

Muninn followed on his twin's tail feathers. "It is confusing."

Together, they bobbed their heads. "You can lose yourself."

CHAPTER 6

I reached out, searching through the cacophony of emotions for the right one. I struggled to keep my mental image of Odin in the forefront of my mind. The silver-blue of the bifrost filled my mind, keeping me from using any of my astral senses to help the process.

Technically, what I was doing was simple. Step into the bifrost. Think about the way your destination feels to you. Pull yourself to that feeling and step out.

In reality, the bifrost cut across hundreds of worlds. The jumble of emotions washing past me was so overwhelming, I kept losing my hold on the feel of my destination. Each time it slipped, I shook myself out of it and started again, pulling at the memories I had of Odin.

A flicker of similarity brushed my consciousness and I latched onto it before I could lose it again. I smooshed it against my thoughts of the All-Father, frowning at the variation that gave it a slightly jarring feel.

Frustrated at the process, I pulled harder, then stepped out of the blinding highway between worlds. Exhausted by yet another exertion of will, I flopped down on the grass, barely seeing what was around me.

I stretched out on my back and closed my eyes for a moment. The grass was soft on my back, and the gentle rushing gurgle of water nearby soothed my nerves. I considered falling asleep right there. But that would be rude to my hosts. And the Norse were pretty hardcore about their host-guest relationships.

After a moment, I rolled over, finally getting a good look at my surroundings. The green grass was trimmed to a soft carpet surrounding a stone-paved garden, complete with benches made of a light tan wood. The plants were beautiful and lush, filling the spectrum of colors, textures and shapes.

I stood up, dread replacing my initial confusion. The center of the gardens was made up of a series of ponds, filled with lilies and lotuses. Orange, white and black shapes darted beneath the water plants.

"Why did I end up here?" I muttered. "It was the feel of Odin, but... not quite right."

"Leave!"

The booming voice told me that I'd not only been discovered, but that the resident had recognized me. He was big on trying to charm people to his side, but we'd already done that song and dance.

I turned to face the old wise man who was actually the most petulant god I'd ever met. "Jehovah. Nice to see you again."

The man curled his lip in a sneer. His hands were crossed under his long white beard, each tucked into the other arm's sleeve. "Liar."

I shrugged. "Much of common courtesy is lies of some degree."

"Why are you here?"

I scowled. "Why did you trick me into coming here?" I countered.

"Trick you?" His face was the picture of offended.

I put my fists on my hips. "I was travelling the bifrost, quite innocently, minding my own business. Then you intercepted me by mimicking my destination." I smirked. "Didn't think I'd figure it out, huh? But you couldn't match the feel of Odin completely, could you?"

Jehovah's face immediately turned to stone. One of his eyebrows quirked up while his lips pressed together. "Only for lack of desire to do so, I assure you," he ground out.

I rolled my eyes. "Look, I'm going to be stuck here until- Well, for a while. I don't want to cause problems. I'm just trying to figure out what's going on with this poison crap. Stop screwing with me, and I won't screw with you, okay?"

Jehovah watched me, expressionless. "Poison? Stuck?" Suddenly his brows rose. "You are... unable to return to your body?"

I shrugged. "So much for you being all omniscient, huh? What, you never met an astral projecting coma patient before?" I rolled my eyes again. "Maybe get out once in a while."

A cold shiver ran down my spine as the deity's lips curled up in an unpleasant smile. "Comatose. How... interesting."

"Why is that?" I swallowed my nervousness, but my voice trembled despite my efforts.

Jehovah shrugged, pulling his hands out of his sleeves. "Just a little gray area," he muttered. "A loophole in the rules."

A thought passed through my mind, and the fourteenth runespell tingled against my chest as I pulled out the knowledge of the gods and the rules that bound them. My breath hitched in my throat, and I turned, sprinting for the bifrost.

The knowledge burned through my mind. A mortal who could not get back to their body was a legal gray area. The rules that kept the gods from interfering with the mortal realm could, technically, harm a mortal who was not fully attached to the mortal realm.

Often such mortals entered some sort of comatose or vegetative state due to actually misplacing their bodies. Like losing your car in a huge parking lot, astral travel meant you could misplace your physical self. It was one of the first hazards you learned to overcome when going astral. Most people did the silver cord trick to keep themselves connected to their physical form, but there were other methods, too.

However, if you couldn't get back to your body quickly- or, better yet, be both physical and astral at the same time, a trick I called bilocation... If you couldn't get back quickly, you might just die in your sleep.

At least, that's what the medical exams would indicate. Instead, you would be permanently separated from your body. In the worst cases, your spirit, or astral self, could be attacked and even destroyed, though that was extremely difficult.

All of this flashed through my mind as I ran. I could hear the laughter rising behind me, a strangely pleasant sound that made my insides curl up. The laughter faded as he spoke. The voice, changing from the smooth creak of the old man, Jehovah, to the oily seduction of Lucifer, simply spurred me on.

"Run from me, Nicola. Run far and run fast. I will chase you like a hound chases a fox. When I tire of chasing you, I will catch up to you. But that will not end our sport. I will keep you forever, and your punishment for crossing me will be eternal. Your pain will be my balm."

I threw myself into the blinding chaos of the bifrost without a moment's hesitation, the laughter returning to follow me across the worlds.

CHAPTER 7

I shivered in the blinding cacophony of the bifrost, cowering in what I imagined was the corner of the interdimensional highway. Now that I'd had time to move past the icy fingers of shock, my stomach threatened to empty itself over the fear.

Ironic, considering my astral body had no stomach to empty. I still felt like dry heaving. Or maybe crying. The impulse felt the same at this stage.

Instead, I focused on my breath moving in and out of my astral lungs. It was more of a mental exercise anyway, and this time I wasn't at risk of hyperventilating. I'd done that a few times in the dark days after... Well, after my time with the Hand, after facing down Hel, after facing down Ran, after taking out people who'd proven to be too much of a threat or risk...

I felt my pulse quicken again as those memories tried to flicker through my mind. Instead, I worked on visualizing Ella and Maria. I pictured the details of their faces, the shapes of their mouths when they smiled, the feathering of their hair on their shoulders. Every detail I could remember I pulled at, bringing it to the fore so I could practically see it.

At last, my breathing steadied, and my heart no longer thrummed in my ears. I tried to move around, but fear shot through me again.

I brought back the visuals and concentrated on the breaths. It took twice more before I could bring myself to proceed with my travels.

I huffed a laugh. I didn't actually know if I was moving along the bifrost, or even if that's how the bifrost worked. Maybe the ribbon was less of a road and more of a string of portals. It didn't matter. It worked, and I was pretty sure Jehovah couldn't hurt me while I was in it.

The thought was almost enough to keep me in the emptiness filled with light and white noise. I shook my head. Even after everything, I couldn't hide from what might happen.

Besides, Odin would keep Jehovah at bay. That was kind of Odin's thing – protecting Asgard from invaders. Or at least, getting Thor to do it.

I took another breath, then focused on the feel of Odin. This time, I waited until the feeling was a match, not some odd variation. With a whole flock of roc-sized butterflies trying to beat their way out of my non-existent stomach, I stepped out of the bifrost into...

It was another field. Not of soft grass this time. It was calf-length standing hay. The yellowed ground cover stretched out on either side of me as far as I could see.

I did notice patches of flattened hay, as though something or someone had been active in each of those areas. It reminded me of the aftermath of a festival or faire, when entire swaths of the ground would be flattened by the traffic, tents and activities.

In front of me, past the field and the small valley between, a tall hill towered over it all with a large, squat building perched on top. People moved around outside, though they were far enough away that I couldn't see what they were doing.

The size of the building made me think it was one of the gods' halls, but I didn't have much frame of reference. Perhaps this was a normal-sized building for one of the lesser gods and not Valhalla.

"You are right," Huginn said, landing just to the right of me.

"It's Valhalla," Muninn finished on my left.

I couldn't help but flinch at their sudden arrival. They both eyed me for a long moment.

"Took the long way?" Muninn asked.

Huginn squawked. "Took a long time."

I sighed. "Yeah, I had a detour. It was... interesting. And I don't want to talk about it yet."

The ravens exchanged a glance, then hopped forward. "Come, come," they chanted.

I lifted my chin a bit and paced after the birds as they hopped and fluttered across the field. I let my legs stretch into long strides as I walked. The grass parted easily for me, and the sun was just warm enough to be comfortable, even with my exertions.

Going down into the valley was easy, but I watched the approaching incline with less enthusiasm. After struggling up the first half dozen steps, Huginn hopped next to me.

"Jump," he said. "Jumping is easy."

"Easier than walking," Muninn agreed, pecking at a stone in front of where he'd landed.

I paused, looking up at the steep hill and then frowning at the birds. "You sure?"

Both of them bobbed their heads, then they flapped away, calling for me to "Jump, jump!"

I shrugged, planting my feet before squatting down a bit, then leaping up as far as I could. I landed with a thud and looked back down the hill in surprise. I'd covered a good third of the climb in one leap.

I turned to squint up at the hilltop and jumped again, then again. Within a few seconds, I'd scrambled the last few feet up and over the ridge.

The lodge was actually huge, sitting along the peak of the hill. The bulge of the peak was reflected in the line of the longhouse, making it appear as if it might be more than a single story tall. Instead, it must have covered several thousand square feet.

The narrow side was no less than 30 feet long, with a huge set of double doors open under an awning that jutted out another ten feet.

Inside, I could see three tables that stretched through the longhouse, disappearing over the bump of the peak.

The walls were lined with benches piled high with blankets and hides. Huge windows were propped open every ten feet. The covers opened up, like a thatched lid with the hinge along the top of the opening. Giant poles held them up to let in air and light.

The people were no less intimidating. Burly men and Amazonian women with wiry muscles all walked around in various states of dress and armoring. Many carried or worked on weapons. I spotted swords, spears, bows and arrows, axes, and more.

To one side, I heard the clanging of a blacksmith's hammer and anvil. Farther away, groups of people appeared to be training with various weapons, repeating moves as individuals or in groups. Some of them seemed to be debating techniques, with animated body language and occasionally using the weapon in their hands to demonstrate something.

One small group sat meticulously pulling apart, cleaning and putting back together some kind of handgun. Another group perched on hide-covered stumps around a beat-up table, drinking from steins and horns, and apparently making each other laugh.

There were others, too. People who were very obviously not warriors moving among the fighters. They carried cups, pitchers glistening with condensation, and platters of food.

The whole thing was very upbeat but overwhelmingly busy. I very nearly turned on my heel to leave. Then I saw Rade.

The Valkyrie strode out of the longhouse, walking purposefully toward a group of people practicing throwing axes. She looked just like she had years ago, when she had drilled me in fighting practice along the Appalachian Trail.

I took a deep breath and approached the group. As I drew near, one of the men noticed me and spoke to Rade. The warrior woman turned and froze.

"Nicola. What are you doing here?" She hurried over to me. "I would have heard if you had died."

I frowned. "You would?"

She gave a half-shrug. "All of us would. We are to keep an eye on you, you know."

"The hero thing? Yeah. Not dead, but close." I shook my head. "I need a place I can rest and recharge."

Rade frowned this time. "Very well. But I would hear your tale."

I nodded, suddenly exhausted. "You will, when I'm not seeing double."

Rade guided me inside and over to a small door at the back of the hall. "We have some private rooms, in case people come here with more... modern sensibilities."

There were several small rooms and she led me into one. It was fitted with a rough daybed piled high with blankets. There was a small rug on the floor, and a two-drawer stand.

Rade gestured me in. "Rest, then come find me. I'll send word to Mercy, as well."

The last was almost a question, so I nodded my approval. Rade closed the door as she left, and I stripped my clothes away with a thought and a push of will.

It would be good to see Mercy again after so long. I hadn't really seen her since...

The thought drifted off and I followed.

CHAPTER 8

Sleeping in spirit form was an interesting thing. Unlike being in a physical body, there were no dreams, no tossing and turning. It was simply a matter of shutting down.

The tricky thing was, even though there was no real physical exhaustion in spirit form, you could still be exhausted. It was similar to the fatigue you could get from a long car ride. Even lying in bed all day was never as draining as sitting in a car. Also, when your consciousness was running around, your body didn't rest as well as it should.

My rest was very much needed, and I took a long one. At least, that's what Rade said when I finally regained consciousness and emerged to search out my Valkyrie friends.

Well, Mercy was a friend at least, I admitted to myself. I'd never really figured out what Rade was to me. Teacher of sorts, maybe even a mentor. She gave me advice and there had been that one joke, but I wasn't sure "friend" was the right category for her.

I walked slowly through the longhouse, admiring the woodwork of the thick oak plank tables and the hide-padded benches that lined them. They were made to be sturdy and functional, and that combined into a rugged aesthetic that was nice.

The wider platforms along the walls were covered with even more hides and a bohemian blend of patterns on the woven blankets. Bits of color popped against the pale, creamy wool. A quick touch told me that the hides were buttery-soft and the blankets plush and without the stiff feel of synthetics or low-quality wool.

The room was warmed by large fires at each end, and the firewood lent a pleasant note to the wood and hide odors. Round loaves of dark bread baking on the hot stones along the edge of the fire and the giant side of meat turning on the spit rounded out the scent. I couldn't tell what was in the cauldron that bubbled gently to one side of hearth, but it also smelled hearty and satisfying.

Outside, I found Rade in light, sparring armor sitting at one of the tables with a few other people dressed similarly, including Mercy. Rade spotted me in the doorway and waved me into a seat at the table. She gestured to one of the servers moving around. He disappeared into the longhouse.

I smiled at Mercy as she leaned over to hug me.

"Nicola! I couldn't believe it when Rade told me you were here," Mercy said. "Before you launch into what I'm sure is a crazy-odd story... This is Bo and Sten, some of our earliest recruits. And Revna, likely the best archer in centuries."

I nodded to the two burly men and the raven-haired woman. "Hey. Um, how's it going?"

Revna smiled. "It goes. We are doing formation exercises today."

I blinked. "Oh. Um, that's... good."

I glanced at Rade. She shook her head. "Battle strategies. Not exactly your thing."

"So tell us this tale," Mercy said.

I nodded and thought for a moment. I rested my elbows on the table, then jerked upright when the server returned. He set down a large stein and a jug, both filled with apple cider.

The drink was joined by a platter of thinly sliced beef, a selection of fruits cut into bite-sized chunks, and a large sheet of a pale-yellow flatbread folded twice over. There was a compote of a spreadable, white cheese and another of dark reddish jam flecked with tiny seeds.

I smiled my thanks and glanced at the others. None of them seemed to be interested in the food, though Mercy gestured for me to eat.

I tore a piece off the lefse bread and folded it over before dipping it into the cheese spread and jam. "Okay, short version is, I went to California for a conference, got roped into joining a meeting to resolve safety issues at a nuclear power plant, and the whole lot of us got poisoned. Now, I'm in a hospital, in a coma." I bit into the tortilla-like potato bread. The spongy texture nearly disappeared under the creamy-sweet taste of the toppings.

The group exchanged looks.

I shrugged. "Saying it out loud makes it sound so much weirder." I popped a berry into my mouth. "Oh, and I ran into Jehovah on my way here. He's gonna hunt me down like a- How did he put it? Like a hound hunts a fox."

Rade choked and the Einjarhar warriors stared with their mouths open.

I cleared my throat. "Yay, me?" I sighed. "Hey, at least if I die, I'm in the right place already."

Mercy shook her head. "No, you aren't supposed to come here."

I frowned. "So I'm not gonna be in Valhalla when the perma-death comes?"

"You wouldn't want to be." Mercy propped her foot up on the bench next to her, wrapping her arms around her knee. "You have your family."

"I get that Valhalla is not the ideal afterlife, but I can't help but feel kinda... insulted."

I tore off another piece of bread. I knew that the food wasn't nutrition for my body. Those needs would be fulfilled by the medical staff at the hospital. This was, literally, food for the soul. It provided metaphorical nurturing and stimulation through sensory pleasures.

Mercy watched me take several more bites before she answered me. "The modern idea of Valhalla being so important is a problem we've had for a while." She leaned on her elbows. "The whole hero thing has never been so revered. Most of us find it pretty off-putting."

I considered that for a moment. "Is that because being a hero would get you killed?"

Mercy nodded. "Heroism is like suicide. Sometimes it happens, but why would you idealize it?"

I laughed. "Yeah, that is definitely not how we view it these days. We have superheroes and movie heroes, and they always win, they always survive, and they always get the girl."

Revna leaned forward. "But you must be special, unique, to be so successful. A demi-god."

I shrugged. "Actually, there's a whole trope about weak losers and everyman types becoming these heroes. Sometimes they are even women." The last was added with heavy sarcasm and a glance at Revna.

Revna scowled at me. "And there are questions about why you modern folk have such a problem with… What are they called? Incels?"

Mercy grimaced and I shook my head. "I get it. We made heroes indestructible, told people anyone could do it, and now we have this idea that heroism is the goal, as well as a means to getting everything you want." I shot a wicked grin at Rade. "Like Valkyries being the love-slaves of Valhalla."

Rade sniffed her chin lifting high. "Ridiculous notions. And sex-obsessed to boot."

Mercy laughed aloud, while I grinned, and the warriors exchanged confused looks.

Finally, Rade stood. "Come, Einherjar. It's time to prepare for the exercise."

They left me and Mercy chuckling into mugs of cider.

"So it really isn't a reward," I muttered, watching a stoic group of swordsmen exchanging blows.

Mercy tilted her head to one side. "Never to see your family again, practice for battle every day, knowing that the result is that you will die trying to minimize the end of all creation? Who would think that was a reward?"

I shrugged, staring down at my mug.

Mercy reached over to clasp my wrist. "Are things going so poorly with your family?" She tried to get me to meet her eyes, but I kept them locked on the wood grain of the table. "Is it just your mother, or are the girls still distanced, too?"

I opened my mouth to respond and, instead of my carefully scripted response, developed over the course of months -- instead, I sobbed.

CHAPTER 9

After crying hard for several minutes, I took a huge swallow of cider. The warmth of Mercy's arm around my shoulders smoothed some of the edges from my sorrow.

"I just don't know what to do," I moaned. "I tried and tried to do the right thing. I really think that, given the shitshow that went down, I did make the right choices. But they hate me for it."

Mercy nodded. "You did what you had to do."

I lifted my face to the sunlight, closing my eyes against the blinding rays. "They can't even tell me what I should have done. They just don't like what I did." I let my head drop down again. "It's not fair."

"Oh, Nicola. I know," Mercy crooned, rubbing my arms in support. "It's the huge con of being the quest-hero."

I nearly rolled my eyes. "What? Dealing with human stupidity? 'Cause it *is* stupid." I set my jaw stubbornly, not sure who might argue but prepared for it.

"It is stupid," Mercy agreed. "Stupid and frustrating. But I meant the part where no one quite gets it." She filled my mug with more cider from the jug. "It goes back to that stuff about idealizing heroes. People get this idea that the hero gets to be clearly right, but that almost never happens."

"Even with Zaro, people criticized how harsh I was with him." I snorted. "I literally watched him attack my baby after he abused me for weeks, then I lost control, and I got shit for that." I flung my hands up.

"What the hell? Should I have just taken it? What is the right answer there?"

Mercy patted my arm. "It isn't about the right answer, Nicola."

"What is it about then?"

"It's about how scared people are that this stuff could happen to them." Mercy folded her arms on the table in front of her, watching me as she spoke. "People want to feel like they have control, like they could handle things better. When faced with a scenario – even someone else's shit – that is too chaotic, they criticize it so they can feel like they wouldn't be caught in a situation where they weren't in control."

I shook my head. "That's not realistic."

Mercy chuckled. "Realistic isn't the goal. Mental security is." She leaned back and stared at me for a moment. "But you know this already, don't you."

I shrugged. "I've heard the concept. I just..." I sighed. "I just wish someone could assure me that other people's judgment for their own self-serving reasons... That it wouldn't hurt me."

The Valkyrie shook her head. "You know I can't do that." She smiled. "I mean, I could, but you respect facts and reality too much for that to be more than a kiss on the boo-boo."

I frowned. "Boo-boo?" My hands went to my hips, despite still sitting. "Boo-boo?!? What in the name of sweet baby Baldr are you trying to say?"

Mercy smirked. "Oh, nothing. I would never imply that you sometimes fall into an emo spiral and turn into the most llama of all drama-llamas."

I stuck my tongue out at her. "You're so mean to me. I should just run away."

The Valkyrie shrugged. "Okay, but then you'll miss the tour." At my raised eyebrow, she continued. "Well, this is but one hall in the lands of Asgard. And Asgard is but one of the Nine Worlds. I thought you might want to see some of the other stuff, too."

I shook my head. "You know me so well." I smacked my hands down on the table. "When do we start?"

"Now?" Mercy shrugged. "Unless you have something better to do...?"

I stood up, stretching out before waving my hand. "Oh, I'm sure I can fit this in."

The Valkyrie made a face before leading me back toward the bifrost. As she walked, her clothing shifted from the traditional light armor to her usual jeans and a flannel shirt.

We approached the bifrost and Mercy grabbed my hand. "It's easier for me to just bring you along than to try to explain how to find the new exit," she said. "But pay attention to how the energy changes so you can find it again."

I nodded and we stepped into the blinding silver-blue light. The white noise filled my ears like ocean waves, and I twitched my fingers, checking that Mercy's hand was still there. She squeezed back reassuringly.

I shifted my focus to the energies flowing around me, like an emotional landscape going past a speeding car. I barely caught whisps of what was passing us, or what we were passing. It was hard to tell if we were what was moving or if the worlds moved around us.

I let the feelings brush against my consciousness, focusing on trying to recognize any of them. The feelings were complex concepts that appealed to entire memories rather than basic, one-dimensional feelings.

I was pretty sure that the soft but tough feeling that reminded me of an old-school warrior princess tinged with deep sorrow was where I'd find Freya and her hall, Sessrumnir, in the fields of Folkvang. The lovey-dovey sense I got along with thoughts of liveliness, pranks and puppy-playfulness and an undercurrent of iron-hard boundaries had to be Freyr and his wife, Gerdr.

I relaxed into the experience, letting the sense-memories tell me where we were, or at least guessing at it. There were so many feelings going by so fast, yet I was sure there hadn't been any repeating. I could feel myself letting go of any judgments about the energies I was sensing. It was just information. There was no good or bad about it. Just information.

Feelings of being held by a loving parent. Feelings of being held by a lover. The exhilaration following good physical exercise. The exhaustion of having lived through a good day with friends and family and safety.

I felt myself falling into that semi-conscious state that often came with meditation. I was drifting, held only by Mercy's hand clutching mine. I tried to keep that lifeline in my conscious thoughts, but it floated away in the wash of energy, pulling my consciousness outward.

My astral body seemed to dissolve, merging with the power of the bifrost, scattering into the thousands of places the bifrost touched.

My free hand tingled, and I jumped back into full consciousness. Something had touched me. I reached out with my energy, trying to find what had brushed against my spirit. Nothing.

I relaxed again for a moment. Something both hot and icy cold grasped my free hand firmly and yanked. My hold on Mercy broke and I hurtled out of the bifrost into darkness.

CHAPTER 10

I stumbled into the thick growth of plant life. Vines tangled around my ankles, and I nearly went face-first into a huge trunk that arched up nearly 10 feet, then back down into the ground. The ropey fibers of the limb and the papery bark left gritty scrapes on my hands when I caught myself.

I looked around, trying to figure out where I'd been flung. I pushed away the shiver of fear that tried to crawl up my spine. The bifrost was nowhere to be seen, but a huge tree loomed several yards away. It was as good a place to go as any.

I carefully picked my way through smaller roots arching up in bows. It would have been easier if I had found a patch of dirt to walk in, but everything seemed to be wood that was just a little too smooth to walk on, covered with damp moss that scraped away to form a slippery mush.

Staggering through the mist and boughs, I wondered where the bifrost was. The branches overhead were too thick to let me see very far. My hope was that I would have some idea of where to go once I reached the big tree. Maybe I could climb the tree, or there would be a break in the canopy. Sighing, I kept up the crawling pace, working hard not to break any astral bones.

The first change I noticed was a tickling prickle on the back of my neck. Immediately, I felt eyes on me.

I stopped scrambling over a particularly large root and whipped my head around. Scanning the foliage behind me, I strained to hear any sign of what might be there. Fear curled in my belly, and telling myself that there was nothing there didn't help.

After a moment, I moved on, slipping and struggling over a nasty tangle that was only a little easier going than the rest of my surroundings. I tried to dismiss the feeling and concentrate on placing my feet securely.

"Niiii-colaaaaa!"

The call was soft and creepy, drifting toward me from the tangle of roots and trunks and vines. I froze.

"Niiii-colaaaaa!"

The soft voice was closer. I was pretty sure it was masculine, so it wasn't Mercy or another Valkyrie looking for me. My eyes darted around, seeking the source of the voice.

"Niiii-colaaaaa!"

I panicked, turning and rolling my whole body over the huge root in front of me. I slipped and caught myself, took several steps, and slipped again. This time, my knee slammed into a root.

Pain shot up my leg, but I pulled myself up. The giant trunk must only be about two yards away. For some reason, I latched on to the idea that reaching the trunk would mean safety.

"Niiii-colaaaaa!"

The voice spurred me on, and I used my hands and arms as much as my legs and feet to get around the tangles of limbs. The huge trunk loomed in front of me, almost within reach. Every time I thought only a few steps would bring me to it, I found there was still a yard or more of tangled roots to cross.

My foot slipped into a space between two roots and wedged itself. I pulled it frantically, but it wouldn't slip out the way it got in. All I got was bruised ankle bones for my trouble.

I reached down and tried pulling on the roots, but they were too tight and thick to move. Finally, I leaned back and kicked at the roots with my other foot, trying to hold myself up with my arms. I kicked my own leg several times before landing enough blows on the root to crack it.

Then someone was kneeling beside me. Delicate but worn hands reached out from under the dark gray cloak. The fingers traced the cracked root, and it shifted, releasing my foot. I pulled it out quickly. When I began to stutter my thanks, the hand gestured for silence.

The hand disappeared into the folds of wool, only to reappear with a small, corked jug. The hands pulled the stopper out and drizzled water onto the root. I stared in shock as the crack sealed up. Within seconds, it looked like it had never been damaged.

The form stood and turned to face me. The questions died in my throat. I knew that face. Perhaps not specifically, but I knew what the lack of discernable age meant when paired with slightly unfocused eyes and aesthetically neutral features.

The woman smiled at me, showing sharp teeth between pale lips. Dust-gray hair showed under the hood of her cloak.

"You know what I am, quest-hero," she said in a voice like wind sighing through dead branches.

I nodded and forced out a single word. "Norn."

*****

The creature led me along a path that seemed to form just for her to walk easily. We rounded the massive trunk, which must have been at least 50 feet wide.

There was a large pool of water with a little spout bubbling up to break the surface, indicating a spring. More woman-like creatures moved around the wellspring, watering various roots, packing mud on the trunk from the edge of the pool, or staring into smaller puddles scattered between the giant roots.

Several of them turned their sightless gazes on me, and I shivered with fear. Each pair of eyes was like a cold, clammy hand on the back of my neck.

"I am just trying to get back to the bifrost-" I began.

The creature leading me met my eyes with hers. Or nearly did. Lifeless eyes the color of road tar focused midway between my eyes and the back of my skull.

"You will meet with Skuld. She will tell you your fate."

The Norn's voice fell on my ears like old paint flecks.

"I thought you guys didn't tell people their fates until it was already locked in..." I swallowed hard as the woman watched me without blinking. Somehow, I just knew she'd been waiting for me to have that realization.

"Come. Skuld awaits."

I hurried to stay close to her, partially because it was easier to walk if I stayed in the wake of the path the roots made for her, but also because she was the scary thing I kind of knew. I was surrounded by scary things I didn't know at all. I concentrated on not meeting anyone's eyes.

I found myself staring into the pool of water. Despite the various activity in and around the wellspring, the surface was smooth and clear as glass.

I watched a Norn dip a small jug into the water to collect it. The ripples spread out from the jug for the space of a handsbreadth, then simply disappeared as if swallowed by the water. A hand landed on my chest, and I looked up into those cold, gray-rimmed black eyes.

"Do not touch the water, mortal."

I blinked and looked back at the water. I was standing at the edge of where the wellspring had muddied the dirt around it. I glanced over the several feet to where we had been walking a moment before.

"What-?"

Something that might have been a distant relative to sympathy crossed her face. "The water draws you in. You must resist. You are not ready to have the knowledge of the Norns."

My hand reached up to touch the Fourteenth Runespell, the one that gave me the knowledge of all gods and god-creatures.

The Norn's eyes flicked down to the pendant, then back to my face. "The knowledge is different. More. You are not ready."

I frowned. "Are you saying I will be someday?"

"Perhaps," she said. "You have many paths you could follow. Many choices to make. That is one. Now, come. Skuld awaits."

I took a step after her, then looked back at the water. Knowledge was a temptation. I shook my head and hurried after the creature. Knowledge was also painful more often than not. I wondered if hesitation over that pain was what made me not ready for the knowledge.

"That is one way to look at it."

I bit back a gasp as I found myself face to face with one of the Norns who had visited me years before.

"You lied to me," I blurted out.

CHAPTER 11

The woman frowned and I swallowed hard.

"You lied to me," I said again, trying for a more moderate tone.

"We did and we did not," the woman said, her voice squishing like viscera. She lounged against one of the roots, draping herself like a corpse, like a sated lover. Her moist, full lips curved into something like a smile. "We told you what would motivate you. The inferences and assumptions were your own."

I shrugged uncomfortably. "Well, yes. And I should have known better than to take what you said at face value. You could teach the fae to bend truth."

Skuld raised an eyebrow. "Who says we did not?" She stood up and slinked over to a small pool of water. "Come, mortal. Let us find truth in what could be."

I stared at her. I'd been half certain she would strike me down for being rude, but, instead, she accepted the accusation as if it were fact. I shook away the thought. She hadn't outright admitted it, so it wasn't fact. Merely more assumption that she was directing, encouraging. I narrowed my eyes and followed the woman.

She squatted beside the pool and gestured to it. "Look, mortal. See what you can see."

I wriggled up against a root to get as far away from the Norn as I could as I squatted next to the puddle as well. "What am I looking at here?"

Skuld shrugged one shoulder. "I do not determine that. Just look."

I leaned over the water and peered down into it. Bright lights flickered behind my eyes and the sound of a thousand voices talking roared in my ears. I couldn't tear my gaze away from the liquid mirror, despite my growing fear.

A split second after it started, the images in the pool released me. I had been trying to pull back so hard that the release sent me flying back against the branches and roots. I groaned, suddenly feeling exhausted. I lay limp in a tangle of thick woody strands, staring up into the vines and branches of the tree.

It suddenly struck me that I must be within the roots of Yggdrasil itself. That was where the Well of Urðr was located. That was where the Norns hung out. Which meant I was staring up at the world tree, an embodiment of no small part of the multiverse.

The awe overcame me for a moment, then washed away as I laughed. "Frickin' multiverse is poking me in the butt," I muttered, shifting uncomfortably. I struggled out of the nest-like tangle and hobbled back over to Skuld and the pool. "So, should I try again or what?"

The Norn looked at me. "Try?" She shook her head with a laugh that sounded like boots stepping in sludge. "You just stared into that pool for three hours. I doubt you'll get more out of it."

I gaped at her. "Three hours? But-" I shook my head. "No, it was only a few seconds. Right? I mean, I didn't really see… anything."

"Such knowledge is not for you to remember yet, though much of it you had already glimpsed." Her eyes bore into me. "I am curious as to how that could happen."

I shrugged. "How would I know? I don't remember any of it."

The Norn was at my side in the blink of an eye, pushing into my personal space without apology. Her narrowed, dead eyes ran over my face and hair, then down my neck.

"Well, well," she murmured, reaching for my throat. "What have we here?"

Her fingers brushed my skin and I felt dirty, lustful and slimy at the same time. I nearly vomited from the conflicting, roiling sensations. I pressed myself back against the roots arching up behind me.

"A memory pearl? Where did you get such a thing?" Her eyes stared into the space about a foot behind my eyes.

I swallowed convulsively. "Uh, I don't-" Then I remembered. "It was during my initial quest. To help me find the first of the Runespells."

She leaned forward, her lips nearly meeting mine. "Tell me who."

"The ravens," I whispered hoarsely. "Please don't hurt them-"

Skuld was suddenly back on the other side of the pool. She waved her hand dismissively as she went back to lounging against the roots of Yggdrasil. "I wouldn't hurt them for that," she said. "They may have hedged a line, but they followed the rules in doing so. You do not have ready or easy access to those memories."

I gulped. "I do not."

"Then they will only help you when you trigger the knowledge. Now, it is time for you to go."

"Go?" I blinked.

"Do you want to stay?" Skuld asked, lifting her head to send a sickly seductive smile my way.

"Uh, no."

The Norn turned and scowled into the distance. "He approaches." She turned back to me. "His past is the key. You must find out more."

"Who-?" I began.

"Niiiiiiicolaaaaa!"

The creepy, familiar voice drifted between the roots.

"Oh," I said. "Him."

Skuld lifted her hand and, not even straining, peeled the bark off a nearby root. I gasped, seeing the silver-blue light of the bifrost within the limb.

"It is time for you to go," the Norn said.

With a nod, I stepped into the bifrost, somehow easily fitting into the two-foot diameter strand the Norn had opened. For a long moment, I struggled to clear my mind of the anxiety I felt about my pursuer. It wasn't easy. The feelings kept sneaking in around the edges of my consciousness.

After what seemed like a long time, I felt something comfortable and protective brush against my mind. I latched on to the feeling and stepped out of the bifrost.

I immediately felt a shiver of anxiety. I'd been trying to clear my mind of the lingering fear of Jehovah, but I knew it had crept in at the last minute. I wondered if that would affect where I'd come out. And, if so, in what way.

I stared in awe at the dense forest of linden tress, birches, and willows. Leaves of reddish-orange, yellow-gold, and yellow-green filled the branches and covered the ground.

In the center of an almost perfectly round glade, a young woman sat crying. Her golden, light brown hair gleamed in the light, and a loose red-gold band peaked between the strands. The woman herself was truly beautiful, and I stood dumbfounded for a long moment.

Finally, she wiped her eyes dry and looked up. "You are Nicola? I have heard much of you."

She held one hand out to the side and let a handful of red-gold drops fall into the leaves.

I took me another moment to put the pieces together. "Lady Freya, it is wonderful to meet you." I hesitated. "I seem to have gotten myself lost."

Freya smiled. "So I see. Come to my hall, and we shall see what we can do about that."

CHAPTER 12

Freya's hall was huge. The overall feel was much like Odin's hall, though with a more laid-back mood. There were still warriors sparring and taking care of weapons and armor, but it was less intense.

Watching several of the pairs fighting, I realized they were more playful, stopping to joke and laugh. Freya stopped to follow my gaze, smiling when two men threw down their swords and began grappling each other like brothers fighting over a TV remote.

I glanced at the goddess. "Not so much pressure to be ready for Ragnarök, huh?"

Freya smiled. "We here at Sessrúmnir are in a rather unique position. The prophecies of Ragnarök do not include us."

My eyebrows raised. "So in a place where everyone pretty much knows how they are going out, you... don't?"

Freya nodded. "My warriors here have the choice to join the einherjar of Valhalla during the last battle. Several have chosen that path and practice for it." She gestured to some of the fighters who were taking their sparring more seriously.

"Others will join the battle, but only as a last line of defense." She gestured to several warriors who were practicing with shields. "And some have decided to be the guardians of whatever gods and mortals survive the battle."

"Including you?" I asked.

Freya shrugged. "Perhaps. The prophecies do not say if I survive. We shall see what happens."

"You are pretty calm about it," I said. "Doesn't not knowing drive you crazy?"

The goddess shrugged as we approached an empty table. She waved a hand for me to sit, and a serving man poured us drinks. "I've had time to come to terms with the ambiguity, though it is annoying." She smiled. "Others have the stability of knowing what their decisions should be. I do not. It seems that is my constancy."

I frowned. "Ambiguity?"

Freya nodded. "Ever since Odr disappeared."

"Your husband."

"He used to return to me infrequently, but he's been gone for nearly 1500 years now." She stared into the distance, her fingers brushing against the golden torc at her neck. "I miss him."

I leaned on the table, propping my head up with my hand. "You loved him?"

The goddess smiled softly. "I still do." The smile slipped from her face. "I just wonder if I am the reason he does not return."

I frowned. "What do you mean?"

Freya shook her head. "Loki likes his rumors, and he likes accusing me of sleeping around."

I watched her, not sure what to say. After all, one didn't simply go around accusing warrior goddesses of playing the field, even if one had no moral issue with such behavior.

Freya caught my expression. "I've had my trysts, but not nearly to the level that the god of mischief claims. He makes it sound like I use my husband's absence as a green light to 'conquer' every god in existence. Twice."

I nodded. "That must be irritating." I thought about the rumors I occasionally caught wind of in my small town. Being a single mother wasn't exactly what those bigoted, nosy jerks considered good moral ground. It was often bad enough that I thought twice before even considering a date. "Really irritating, actually," I grumbled.

Freya sighed. "Odr had wanderlust and jealousy. Those were his only real flaws. When Loki started talking smack, Odr's trips got… longer. Sometimes I wonder if I chased him away." The goddess's eyes glistened with golden tears.

I nodded my understanding. "So you cry for him and for the relationship you don't have."

Freya smiled sadly. "Tears of amber and gold, the blood of my broken heart."

Her words tugged at my memories. "Why do you cry amber?" I asked.

The goddess leaned forward. "When we first married, Odr was wonderful, attentive, loving. If something made me cry, he would catch the tear on his finger, and it would turn into amber. I don't know how he did it." She shrugged. "I guess it just… happens that way now. But only when I cry over him."

"Hmm." I frowned trying to bring up the tickle in my mind. But the more I pulled at it, the more I knew I wasn't going to be able to bring it back. I shook my head in frustration.

"Nicola," Freya said finally. "I'm glad you are here, and you are welcome at my hall any time. But why are you here now?"

I shrugged. "I was supposed to tour the halls and worlds with Mercy, but something… I don't know. I got pulled out of the bifrost, I guess. I'm not sure if that's right, but that's how it felt."

"It pulled you out here?"

"No, first I ended up within the roots of Yggdrasil, near the Well. I had an interesting run-in with the Norns. Skuld, actually."

Freya's eyebrows lifted. "Really? She's rather reclusive."

"Yeah. She made me look into a puddle, then showed me the door. She said it was stuff I needed to remember, but I don't remember any of it."

The goddess nodded. "That happens with the waters of the Well." She shot me a curious look. "So she didn't give you any prophecies?"

I shrugged. "I think puddle vision was supposed to be a prophecy, but, like I said. Zero remembering. I just don't know."

Freya watched me for a long moment then nodded. "That's the way it goes sometimes."

"It's frustrating as hell," I muttered.

She laughed, a sound like bells. Not the tinkling kind, but the full, rich sound of church bells. "Yes, it is. Dealing with gods and fae are both great ways to learn patience."

I shot her a raised eyebrow.

She shrugged. "Just because I'm a part of one or both groups doesn't mean I can't have a little self-awareness." She grinned. "Let me show you around a bit, then we'll see if we can't find that errant Valkyrie."

I stood up. "She takes so much looking after."

The goddess grabbed my hand, and we walked like old friends across the field called Fólkvangr, telling each other stories about our lives.

CHAPTER 13

"Nicola!"

Mercy's voice brought us around. We had been all around the field and even peeked into the hall, before pausing to talk. Freya was an excellent and entertaining hostess.

Mercy hurried up and did a double take when she caught sight of Freya's face.

"My lady Freya!" The Valkyrie actually gave a little bow. "I apologize for intruding on your domain-"

The goddess waved a hand. "I am not so strict as that, warrior. You need not stand on formality."

Mercy blushed. "Of course. I was just searching for..." She cut her eyes to me. "Well, I seem to have misplaced my quest hero."

I snorted. "Misplaced? Me? I'm not misplaced. I'm placed exactly where I should be." I grinned. "That's the fatalistic side of me coming out. 'Cause of my life-changing encounter with the Norns, and all that."

Freya laughed while Mercy frowned.

"That was years ago," the Valkyrie said.

I looked at my left wrist, knowing I wasn't wearing a watch. "Nope. About half an hour. I'm sure of it."

Mercy blinked. "What have you been up to?"

I smiled, waving to Freya and grabbing Mercy to drag her away. "You just can't leave me alone for a minute! Now, come on. I've gotten the tour here. What's our next stop?"

Mercy shook her head. "You do manage to bowl over every expectation we have of you, you know that?"

I grinned as we approached the bifrost. "I do my best."

I gave her a little push and let her grip on my hand pull me into the interplanar highway behind her.

The blinding light was becoming more familiar. It was still a bit nerve wracking, but not to the point that it bothered me. In fact, except for the fact that my trips in the bifrost kept going askew, it was almost pleasant.

I let the emotional energy of the worlds wash over me. It charged me up in a way, making me feel connected and powerful. It was like I could reach out and become any of the places, any of the people, anything at all.

My energy reached out at the thought, and I let myself feel the tendril seeking a new form. With all the feelings rushing around me, I felt strangely detached.

That was the red flag. Detachment in the spiritual realms was never a good thing. Detachment from feelings, detachment from self, could lead to detachment from the body. With my current situation, any further separation could be the broken strand that killed me.

I wrenched myself under control, snatching back the tendril and grasping for an emotional connection that would bring me back from the brink. I thought back over the past years and gasped. There was only one thing that kept me anchored. Well, technically two things. My daughters.

It shocked me to my core. Had my life really become so chaotic and full of harsh realities and pain that I only had them to live for? Or was it just that they were the most important?

I dug through my memories, searching through slices of my life. Going to Indianapolis only to fail to save Muriel. Sure, I'd gotten her away from the situation, but it was more like I'd chased her away, ruined the life she had built. I hadn't saved her in any real way.

Before that, my mother had been someone I cared about, but we never understood each other. After, there had been a chasm in our relationship that I couldn't breach. I wondered if she had even tried.

The Hand of Asclepius was where I had intended to secretly infiltrate a cult. Only I'd gotten sucked into it, hardcore. I'd completely lost control – several times – before the end. In the end, Bob had gotten revenge on me through Zaro. My baby's throat sliced in my own backyard, and a complete loss of any humanity when I fully berserked for the first time.

That had been the first violation of my family that came directly from my quest. My mother had known enough to blame me, and Ella had been too young to understand the nuances of it all. However, all of that had been secondary to embracing Maria as a new member of the family.

Then I'd gone on vacation to hike the Appalachian Trail with Joseph. It hadn't been my choice, but I'd understood why Joseph had chosen it. Back to nature was a default cure for what ails us in the Pagan community.

There had been no way for him to know that our fun little trip would turn into a manhunt and a race for the fate of humanity. Specifically, we had to stop a monster from being released upon the world.

There had been a lot of moral gray area in that one. The monster, after all, hadn't done anything... yet. But even he didn't deny that he would. After everything was said and done, I had come away from that by keeping an innocent imprisoned and straight up murdering my long-time nemesis.

So who was the monster, really?

Another attempt at a vacation lead to another disaster when my cruise to reconnect with mom and the girls sank. Literally.

Once again, I'd ended up physically broken and trying to help. But, unlike before, no one had wanted my help. I'd very nearly estranged our saviors by trying to be their savior, and the whole thing ended with another moral quandary.

Those moral issues had given my mother the motivation to act. My trip home had ended with a tense encounter with child protective services, and nearly a year of me avoiding my mother as much as I could.

I knew the girls resented that, and I felt guilty about keeping them from their grandma. I just couldn't resolve the toxic prejudice she had against me now to allow them to spend time with her. It wasn't fair to any of them, or me, and it wore on me.

The funny thing was that, legally, there was nothing wrong in my life. But all the crap that kept happening was, in my mother's eyes, my fault. And her comments about it were making the girls start to feel the same way.

My only hope and love were my daughters, and I was losing them. The emotional realization of what I'd long suspected hit me like a ton of bricks, and a jerking pull on my hand flung me out of the bifrost.

I fell to my knees, choking on the sobs. Mercy stared at me in shock and confusion while I simply started crying.

"Nicola, are you okay?" The Valkyrie knelt beside me and watched me struggle to respond coherently.

Finally, I shook my head.

"This is the second time you've broken down crying when I'm around," Mercy said, wrapping her arms around me in a comforting, big-sister kind of hug. "I'm going to get a complex.

CHAPTER 14

I finally managed to tell Mercy what happened and why I was crying, though she still seemed a bit confused by it all.

"Is it that you miss Ella and Maria?" she asked.

I shook my head. "I do, but that's not it. I realized I have nothing else in my life. If I didn't have them, I would have nothing to live for. That's how pathetic I've gotten."

Mercy frowned at me. "Pathetic? Why do you say it's pathetic? It's definitely sad, but you're implying it's a failing on your part."

"Isn't it?" I sniffled. "I've pushed away my mother, my best friend, pretty much everyone I know, to the point that I only see people every couple of years most of the time." I wiped my eyes on my shirt, an interesting aspect of the manifestation of emotions and experiences in the spirit realm. "My own mother doesn't want to see me. She only talks to me because she wants time with the girls."

Mercy scowled at me. "That's her failing, not yours."

"None of them understand why I've made the choices I have, and I can't figure out how to explain it to them." I frowned. "It's literally an experience you have to live through to understand, but I wouldn't wish it on anyone."

Mercy nodded. "I know. I've watched other quest heroes before you. Most of them go through this same thing. It's hard to watch it, because they are usually good people with lives worth having." She sighed. "The quest just screws it all up. It screws up the people involved the worst."

I shot her a look. "That isn't reassuring." I smiled a bit. "Destined to suffer. That's me. But I refuse to wallow. Well, at least not right now."

I scrambled up and looked around. The ground was covered in a delicate leafy moss, soft and spongy to walk on without being too soft to move easily.

We were surrounded by trees. It reminded me of the roots of Yggdrasil. Only, where there had been only ropey branches and rough roots with vines and sprigs of green everywhere, here there were leaves and bushes, flowers and grasses.

It was green everywhere, broken only by the shades of brown and tan and even white of bark, and splashes of color in spots where the flowers bloomed wild. Several of the trees held tiny purple berries, and one boasted yellow and red apples. I saw scarlet berries on a cluster of bushes running up a shallow rise.

This was no cultivated garden, like Jehovah's stomping ground. The plants were not organized by type or color, or anything that I could tell. Some plants grew in clusters, some were separated by several yards. This was nature run amok in a fruitful, bounteous display.

"So where are we?" I asked. I suspected the answer, but I didn't want to assume.

Mercy stood beside me and smiled. "You like it?"

I nodded.

"Welcome to Vanaheim, home to the Vanir."

I stared at the lush greenery and nodded again. "Wow. Nature gods, then?"

"Somewhat," Mercy said.

I caught her eye with a questioning look. "Because the Vanir aren't Aesir, they aren't technically gods?"

She nodded. "That's the cliff's notes explanation, yes. But it's actually a bit more complex." She began walking through the overgrown forest and I followed. "Frigga is the goddess of the home, but it's more like she's the goddess of the organization and structure of running a household."

I nodded my understanding and took the next logical leap. "The Jötun and Vanir are aspects of nature, but the Vanir and Aesir are aspects of society, right?"

She nodded. "The Jötun are the primal elements. The Vanir are the more complex natural world and simple, peaceful social concepts, like trade and wealth or bounty."

"Plants, animals, sex and money," I listed. "And the Aesir are the even more complex and aggressive social stuff? Like politics and wars?"

"Exactly," Mercy grinned.

"So what about the Jötun and Vanir who have been adopted into the Aesir?" I asked. "Like Skadi and Frigga?"

Mercy paused and looked around, as if trying to remember where to go. "Jötun are adopted in when they earn it. Skadi is the goddess of winter and snow, but that expanded and grew into things like hunting during the winter, snowshoes, and stuff like that."

"So the Jötun start out as something pretty simple and primal and natural, but then became a more complex social concept."

"Yes." Mercy started off again and I hurried after her.

"That makes sense," I said. "From an objective standpoint, but what happens to the gods themselves."

Mercy shot me a look. "Do you not grow as you move through life? Most of the time, you simply add layers of yourself in pretty much the same themes. Sometimes, though, you have something big and life changing. And you have a more radical shift in who you are."

She ducked through a tangle of trees. "From an 'objective standpoint,' you don't change a lot. You seldom do a complete 180. But sometimes, what starts out as a hard left becomes a 180 as the years layer that change on."

I considered that for a moment. "It's true. Even big changes start out with a more apologetic kind of shift. Next thing you know, you've completely changed your opinion, but over the course of a decade of experiences."

Mercy nodded. "The gods and such aren't really that different. Even we Valkyrie have grown through our experiences, even if that growth is mostly Odin's growth through us as aspects of him."

I shook my head. "That's a confusion waiting to happen." I laughed. "I guess I still don't have the Asgardian mindset."

Mercy laughed. "It isn't easy for mortals to really understand how the gods are. Most understanding is more... intuition than knowledge."

I felt the Fourteenth Runespell tingle against my chest. "The Vanir fought a battle with the Aesir to a draw. The Aesir started it with the way they treated Gullveig. As a result, as compensation, the Vanir demanded equality to the Aesir in terms of godhood."

Mercy nodded. "Several of the Vanir weren't happy about that. Odin believes that's why Freya's husband stays away."

"Odr? Freya thinks it's her fault." I frowned. "I suppose when politics are involved, there's plenty of fault to go around, though."

Mercy nodded and pushed aside a large branch and led me through the thick brush behind it. We emerged onto a field of wildflowers filling the huge valley.

CHAPTER 15

Birds and butterflies swept around in their playful flights. On the edges, I could see deer, elk and other animals frolicking in the shadows where the trees overhung the meadow. We walked out into the bright, warm sunlight, and I let my head fall back, enjoying the heat of the rays on my face. When I opened my eyes again, Mercy was watching me with a small smile.

"It's nice to see you enjoying the little things again, Nicola." She glanced over the valley. "It seems to be a good day today."

"A good day?"

Mercy nodded. "The Vanir are the gods of nature, not the gods of animated musicals based on fairy tales."

I looked around. It was beautiful. The way nature should be seen.

I frowned at the thought. That wasn't how nature was, though. Those deer were on someone's menu eventually. The birds hunted the insects. The trees grew tall on the decaying bodies of the animals. I remembered seeing a video showing a deer actually snatching a bird out of the air and eating it for nutrients it didn't get enough of from its herbivore diet.

Nature was beautiful, yes. But it was also violent, bloody, and a great cycle of things consuming each other. These moments of beauty were stolen times between life and death.

I nodded at Mercy. "So no vicious hunting is going on. Got it."

Mercy grinned. "Well, no hunting here. And, more importantly, no hunting of us."

"Us?" I swallowed hard. I hadn't even considered that. I'd fallen into the typical human mindset of being above and disconnected from nature. I looked around, suddenly afraid. "Uhh."

"We'll be fine," Mercy assured me, heading across the valley. "Just let your instincts tell you when danger is near."

I grimaced. "My instincts are currently being overshadowed by my sudden anxiety." I jumped as we startled a snake hiding among the flower stems and grasses. It slithered away so quickly, I barely saw more than a movement near the ground and grass shifting in its path.

We came to the top of a rise, and I looked down to where the meadow sloped toward the shore of a huge lake. There were large hillocks everywhere along the slope.

Mercy made a beeline for one of the hillocks closest to the shoreline. As we drew closer, I realized I hadn't had any good perspective for how large they actually were. We rounded the bulge and found an opening facing the water.

My eyes widened. "It's a hobbit hole!"

The Valkyrie laughed. "More or less, yes."

She reached out and rapped her knuckles against the wood frame of the opening. There was no actual door, but the frame would keep the dirt from caving in at the entrance.

"Enter!" a voice came out of the darkness within the hillock.

We stepped into the shadows and followed the hallway with what little ambient light there was and by simply running a hand along one of the walls. After a handful of steps, Mercy pushed a leather cover aside.

"Welcome to the home of the First Völva. Heidr, this is Nicola, völva and quest-hero. Thank you for allowing us in your home. Your generosity is bountiful." She bowed slightly to the woman sitting next to the fire.

I blinked and stuttered. "Your generosity is bountiful."

The woman turned milky white eyes on me. I knew she was blind, but I also knew her sight was more of the energetic kind. Despite being a spirit being in a spirit world, I hadn't felt like my soul was stripped bare until this woman's gaze landed on me. Not even Skuld's piercing gaze left so little unseen.

I shifted uncomfortably. The silence drew out, increasing the feeling. It was a technique I was familiar with, but I still had to fight the urge to start blabbing under those piercing eyes.

Mercy watched the exchange calmly. It was a little reassuring that she didn't seem to feel she had to step in, but I still wanted her to do just that. I wanted the woman distracted from watching me for even a second.

Tension built in my shoulders while I wrestled with my self-control. There was nothing I could say that would be appropriate, but I still wanted to admit any and all sins. I wanted to justify my choices. I wanted to prove myself to be a good person so she would just stop staring.

What I really wanted, above everything else, was to explain my relationship with my mother. Could I convince this woman that I deserved sympathy? I wanted her on my side, not on the side of anyone who might judge me harshly. There were too many people I feared would judge me harshly. There had been too many who already had judged me harshly.

Tears filled my eyes as the emotions hit me. I just wanted someone to care, to give me the unconditional love everyone craved. My mother didn't seem to care about me like that anymore. It wasn't fair. I was a good person. Not perfect, but not deserving of that kind of harsh-

I shook myself, recognizing the self-pitying spiral I was going down. Sure, I had the right to those feelings, but what I was doing was more like excusing and justifying everything over someone else's behavior.

I couldn't make people be better, but I could accept that they were wrong and not just feel sorry for myself. I was a quest hero, after all. I was destined to be broken for the good of the world.

I could follow through on my threat to Odin so long ago. I could simply refuse to pursue the Runespells. Maybe. But could I accept the consequences of that? Would those consequences be okay to me?

If I hadn't gotten the First and Second Runespells from Zaro and Nancy, could I have lived with them continuing to abuse people through their cult? If I had let Fenrir be released, would I have been okay with the rampage he'd promised to go on? If I had allowed Ran to get her vengeance instead of finding the Ninth Runespell, would my family have escaped unharmed? And what about the people I'd met on the island?

So many of the deaths on my hands had gotten there to prevent even more deaths on my conscience. Was that an exchange I was okay with?

I remembered what Tyr had said. He had given up his hand to trap Fenrir. But, more importantly, he'd given up part of his reputation. Even not knowing for sure, he had accepted that price. He did not regret it. The risk had been too great.

It was an acceptable exchange. It sucked, but I would make the same choices again if I had to. I probably would have to. But there it was.

"Welcome, Nicola," the woman's voice cut through my thoughts.

The sound was soft but seemed to be power itself. I shivered.

She continued, "You are not what I expected, quest hero."

"Oh?"

She smiled softly as she gestured to the chairs sitting in front of her. "Sit, child, and let us talk of heroism and worth."

CHAPTER 16

I thanked Heidr for the tea and took a sip, ignoring the burns on the woman's hands. I could see the same scars on her neck. The tea steadied my nerves. The emotional rollercoaster had taken a toll.

Mercy sat beside me, and the three of us were clustered around the hearth fire. Mercy seemed quite comfortable, while I kept fidgeting with my cup. Heidr simply sat, occasionally sipping her tea or stirring the pot over the fire. It smelled like fish and herbs.

The völva's dress was a natural tan fabric in the style of old Norse, with an overdress of blue. The overdress was essentially a pair of rectangles held together by two straps over the shoulders and a belt of large, decorated discs joined by chain links. The jewelry and embroidery on the edges were simple but elegant. A sheepskin lay over her legs and several more were scattered across the floor.

"You wanted to speak," Heidr said at last. "Earlier. But you didn't."

I shrugged. "I don't like just talking to fill silence. Even when that makes me uncomfortable."

The woman nodded. "It takes strength of spirit to resist the need to fill the impatient silence. Doing so shows will and patience, as well as self-awareness."

I shrugged uncomfortably. "I guess."

"You are uncomfortable with your role. Finding the Runespells is something you feel is worth it, but you aren't yet convinced you should have that responsibility."

I frowned but she held up her hand before continuing.

"It isn't that you think you cannot do it. You don't understand why others think you can do it."

Mercy shot me a look. "You doubt we see your worth?"

I shrugged. "It happens. A lot."

The first völva continued. "You also fear it is inappropriate due to your role as a mother."

"Why wouldn't I? I'm expected to put my life in danger, to walk a moral tightrope. How am I supposed to raise my kids with any kind of security with that always hanging over my head?"

I felt the anger rising along with the volume of my voice. "I just wanted to give Ella a good life. A simple, stable life. A foundation from which she could become the best version of herself. Instead, she's been nearly killed by you damned gods or your damned followers twice!"

I blinked, realizing I'd risen out of my chair and was leaning forward with fists clenched. I forced myself to relax my hands and sit back down.

"I'm sorry," I muttered.

Heidr waved a hand, dismissing my apology. "You have a lot of anger about this. I wasn't sure." She turned her sightless eyes to Mercy. "The love and guilt overpower the pride, and her resentment overshadows her sense of accomplishment."

Mercy glanced at me before taking a drink, then staring into her cup.

I met the völva's eyes. "So what? My obligation is to do this thing. I will do it to the best of my ability. But I have to balance that with my obligation to my girls. And I try to put them first." I sighed. "It's just that this Runespell stuff gets out of hand so fast."

"Like now?"

I nodded, but I'd been thinking about the cave along the Appalachian Trail. I was thinking about how a puppy had turned into a monster with nothing more than a prophecy and other people's expectations to drive that change. Well, and a couple centuries of isolation.

I was thinking about how simply keeping that monster where it was had resulted in a broken nose, cracked eye socket, and half my hair pulled out. I'd faced death herself. I'd killed. All to keep an innocent monster locked up, just in case.

"It's the moral 'out of hand' that really gets me," I admitted.

Heidr nodded, ignoring the fact that I'd skipped over contextualizing my words. Mercy frowned as if confused. I watched her for a moment, expecting her to give me some of the usual reassurances. She simply stared back as if she'd missed the exchange with the old woman.

The völva leaned forward and patted my knee. "That balance is the hardest to deal with," she said.

I sighed, nodding. The fact that I was being understood was a huge weight off of me. I felt lighter, though I sagged into my seat. I could feel the strain falling away.

"It will get worse." Heidr said. "Much worse."

The heavy feeling crashed back onto me. I nearly groaned aloud. Instead, I raised my head, sorrow pulling at me while I tried to read her expressionless face.

"I am sorry for that," she added. "You do not deserve what is coming, but it is coming all the same."

Mercy shifted. "Perhaps it's time for us to move on. We've taken enough of your time, Lady Heidr."

The white-eyed woman reached out, moving like a snake striking. Her fingers dug into my arm as she clung to me. She exerted inhuman strength to leverage the limb to keep me sitting. "Remember the words of the beast. It is chained in body, not in mind. Its memory is longer than we realize, and it roamed much before it was imprisoned."

I pulled futilely at her hand. "W-what are you talking-?"

She leaned forward, hissing into my face. "It knows where the missing god went. It knows where the liar god came from."

She released me suddenly and I shoved back away from her, causing the chair to slide across the floor. I stumbled as I scrambled farther away only looking back when I reached the leather-covered doorway. Mercy was coming toward me, a concerned look on her face. Heidr sat in her chair, calmly stirring the pot over the fire.

I shook my head and hurried out of the hobbit-hole dwelling. It no longer felt cute and comfy, but rather claustrophobic and... It was like I could feel the bugs and worms in the dirt crawling and writhing around me.

I burst out into the sunshine, trying not to squirm and brush myself off. After all, the grime was mental, spiritual and emotional, not physical... or astral, as the case was.

Mercy was right on my heels. "Nicola? What is it?"

I gasped, trying to get my emotions, my panic, under control. "Did you miss what just happened?" I snapped. Tears burned in my eyes, though I couldn't tell if they were from sorrow, anger, or hurt.

"Yes, actually," Mercy said. She reached out and gently touched my shoulder, as if calming a wild animal. "Heidr can hide things from people. I don't know what happened during most of your conversation, only bits that she allowed me to see and hear."

I dropped onto the soft grass and looked up at the Valkyrie. "What? How?"

Mercy shrugged. "Heidr was once the queen of the Vanir, Gullveig. Not a queen who ruled, a queen who was cherished." She dropped down beside me, rubbing my back as she spoke. "Odin invited her to Asgard. He knew she was the key to dominion over the Vanir."

The Fourteenth Runespell tingled on my chest. "He killed her. Three times, he ran her through and burned her to death. And still she lived, defying him." I smirked at Mercy. "Girl after my own heart."

Mercy laughed. "Yeah. So the overt attack is what set off the war between the Aesir and Vanir. Odin believed the Aesir would win easily, but it was not so."

I reached for the pendants around my neck. My fingers found the Fourteenth easily. "He was kind of a dick before he went to the Well of Urdr, huh?"

Mercy grimaced. "Yeah. See Gullveig was goddess of wealth and money, and she transformed into Heidr-"

"Wealth became knowledge," I mused, staring into the lake before us. After a moment, I shook myself out of my thoughts and snorted a laugh. "Subtle, that."

Mercy nodded and stood with a grin. "Come on. We've only been to three of the Nine Worlds. There's still a bunch left."

I scowled as I let her pull me to my feet. "Yeah, but we have the worlds of fire, ice, death, and darkness left."

Mercy's grin grew wider. "And monsters!"

I stared at her with an expression of concern. "And I'm the one in therapy?"

"Yup!" She pulled me along as we headed back to the bifrost. "Now, let's grab some branches and move on."

"What?" I was sure I'd misheard the Valkyrie. "Branches?"

CHAPTER 17

We stepped out of the bifrost into a hellscape. The ground was made of crumbling black rock and dust. The air choked with sulfur and burning ash.

"Muspelheim," I murmured.

Mercy nodded.

The heat was intense, scalding exposed flesh. I could feel my lips cracking and the moisture being sucked out of my eyes. The sky was dark with a reddish hue that wavered with the effects of heat illusion.

We stood on the side of a mountain, near to where the sides sloped into a valley between other mountains. There seemed to be no flat areas, just craggy peaks, dusty slopes, and occasional chasms cutting through the ground.

Several of the peaks glowed red, as well as each of the chasms, indicating the presence of magma. Ash spewed from hundreds of vents, adding to the pollution of the air.

We began walking, focusing on our footsteps. Our arms were full of branches, which made walking more difficult. One limb in particular was digging into my side, but I couldn't shift the load enough to make it stop.

The choking air didn't allow for easy conversation. Instead, we simply gestured when we needed to communicate anything. Usually, it was Mercy pointing out where to go around a lava-filled crack in our path.

Soon my skin began to darken, then peel back. In shock, I grabbed Mercy and showed her my arms. She only nodded and showed that hers were cracking and peeling the same way.

I figured by her unconcerned reaction, it must be a temporary effect of Muspelheim and nothing to worry about for now. However, I couldn't help but rub my fingers along the peeling skin.

It must have been an hour that we walked, crossing chasms with so much heat rising from them, I could have spread out my shirt and glided on the drafts. We moved around the base of the mountains when we could, crossing smaller slopes when we couldn't.

Finally, we rounded a jutting cliff at the base of a particularly large mountain. Its peak sputtered with ash and sparks, which concerned me enough that I kept glancing up at it. As if knowing it was blowing would give us enough time to escape.

I nearly laughed at that and ended up coughing and choking instead.

As we cleared the cliff, a figure appeared with flesh of molten red and scaley black rock. His eyes were flames and his beard was flowing lava. In his hand was a sword of fire and, where he touched the rock of his seat, sparks flew.

Next to him was a feminine form much like his, with lava hair flowing over her naked chest down to her waist. Her eyes were also flame, but, where his were orange-red, her fires were white-blue.

They sat in twin seats, barely more than mounds of semi-hardened lava, which seemed to refresh with the molten rock from a source beneath them. Surrounding the pair of them, the rock itself burned with flames of orange, red and blue. The whole scene shimmered with heat waves, making the fire beings appear as if in water.

As we came into sight, four flame eyes latched on to us. I shivered despite the heat. These creatures were nothing that I could even hope to face down.

I glanced at Mercy. What was she doing, bringing me here?

She lifted her arms, filled with branches that had dried to a crisp in the hot air. "A gift to you, Surtr, and to your lady wife, Sinmara. May they feed your flames for a time to honor your dominion."

She flung the branches into the flames between us and the fire giants. I stared for a moment then shook off the awe.

"To honor your dominion," I repeated, throwing my own armload down to be consumed in the fires.

Both fire giants closed their eyes as if enjoying the branches burning. It almost looked as if they enjoyed the heat, but their own heat was greater than the flames from those bits of wood. After a moment, I decided it must be like eating for them. And they found the meal to be good. At least they weren't trying to "eat" us.

The fire giants opened their eyes and looked down at us. Surtr's mouth opened, and the roaring and crackling of the fire within him seemed to form words.

"Your gift is good. The woods of Vanaheim feed us well. What purpose is your visit? It is not yet time for the Great Battle."

"It is not," Mercy agreed. "We are simply exploring the worlds and seeing the wondrous variety that exists within them. A small quest but noble, if I dare to say."

Sinmara opened her mouth. The roaring of the flames was somehow softer than that of Surtr. "Noble, indeed, that all worlds be seen as valued. Too often we are dismissed by others."

Surtr shifted. "Mortals dismiss us while treasuring the gifts we gave them. When they cease to respect those gifts, the fires turn on them and destroy what mortals have created instead. This is the penalty; this is justice."

"I am mortal, but I do not speak for all mortals," I said. "In my own experience, I can assure you that many mortals do honor the flames. We are a small following, but we treasure the fire for its mystery and wonder."

Surtr and Sinmara turned to face me fully. Sinmara's lighter voice formed the words I heard. "This is good. We approve of the respect given." She paused for a moment. "Do you enjoy our realm?"

I tried not to cough as I breathed in to speak again. "I admit it is not friendly to my form, but it has a stark beauty that I cannot deny."

Surtr spoke now, a kind of humor coloring the crackle of his words. "Well spoken, mortal, giving praise without lying outright."

I gave him a wry smile. "It does no good to lie to beings such as yourselves. You may appreciate the praise, but you have no real need of it."

"True words, mortal."

Sinmara shifted, drawing my attention. "A gift to the mortal with the sap-sweet tongue: The bitterness of brothers lasts long. Among the gods, it lasts longer. Such rivalry can create followings that no one could foresee or take over followings that no one remained to lead."

I blinked, trying to follow her words, but they made no sense. After a moment, I realized I should respond to her gift, confusing as it was. "I shall remember your words, and I will seek the knowledge within them."

Sinmara nodded, turning away. Surtr simply stared at us while Mercy bade the fire giants farewell. Her hand on my arm brought me back to the moment, and I followed her away from the creatures that ruled the hellish fire world.

"Time to move on, quest hero," she said, grinning.

A crack opened in the ground only feet away from us. I stared into the molten, red rock. The hissing and crackling of the heat filled my head for a moment. I thought I could hear a smooth, seductive voice calling my name.

Mercy touched my arm bringing me back to the present. Her concerned expression was just the kindness I needed. I smiled reassuringly at her.

"Time to move on," I sighed, coughing a little. "I hope the next stop is a bit cooler."

Mercy laughed, but I suspected I would not find the joke amusing once I got it.

CHAPTER 18

We stepped out of the bifrost into a hellscape, though it was inverse to the previous one. The air was just as dry, choking and filled with particles. These particles were, this time, snow and ice.

Snow covered the landscape in white patches and the land was as dry and barren as before. Not even dead trees existed here. Nothing could grow in the intense cold and constant night of Niflheim.

A huge band of pure ice cut across the land, the frozen river, Élivágar, which existed before anything else in the void of Ginnungagap. The surface was so flat from the bitter winds that the bifrost reflected off it, creating the only light in the realm.

As I stared out into the dark landscape, shapes moved around the hills in the distance. Some flowed like black silk while others moved with jerky, stumbling motions.

"What is this?" I choked out.

Mercy shrugged. "You didn't like the heat."

I glared at her. "So you got me out of the kitchen, the house, the neighborhood, and probably anything that resembled humanoid habitation."

She grinned and shrugged again. Waving a hand at the snow-patched rocks, she confirmed my assumption, "Welcome to Niflheim."

I shivered in the cold and hugged my arms. "Okay, where to in this frosty wonderland."

"Well, that's the interesting thing," Mercy said. "The only ones here are the dead. Not sure there's anyone you really want to talk to."

I nodded. "Right. Hel runs this place, as well as Helheim."

Mercy nodded as she began picking her way down the slope. "Technically, they are two parts of the same realm, but then we'd only have eight worlds, and that feels unbalanced. After all, there are upper, middle and lower worlds, and the first two have three each."

I snorted, following the Valkyrie. "So y'all have nine worlds only because... math?"

Mercy laughed. "I didn't say that, but I didn't say that's wrong, either."

We continued along the path of least resistance for several minutes, saving our breath to clamber over rough slopes and trudging through pockets of deep snow. We were so busy focusing on our feet that we missed our surroundings until we stopped for a moment to catch our breath.

I caught the first flicker out of the corner of my eye. I turned to see what had moved and gasped. Mercy followed my gaze to find dozens of shadowy figures converging on us.

"Oh," she said.

"Are we in trouble?" I asked.

She swallowed. "I-I don't know. Not many come here, and fewer talk about it."

We huddled together as the spirits of the dead came closer. They looked dry and lean, as if they were starving. What clothes we could see on them were tattered rags and fluttering bits.

One of the creatures reached for me. I shrank back, unsure of what their touch would do. The fingers passed through my arm, leaving a trail of numbness and cold spreading out. After a moment, though, it faded, and I sighed my relief.

"Quest hero," one whispered, barely audible.

The others echoed its words in a cacophony of soft murmurs, hisses and sighs.

"Me? What do you want with me?" I looked at Mercy, but she shrugged, not knowing anything either.

They continued to speak with the echoing effect, which forced me to concentrate to figure out what they were saying. "We know what you seek. What you will seek. What you have sought."

My nerves kicked into overdrive, and I fell back on my normal defenses. "Oh, great. The dead can conjugate." Mercy nudged me with her elbow, and I rolled my eyes. "Sorry. What is it I am, will be, or was seeking?"

"You seek the missing one. You do not know it yet. You have found him, and he seeks you. Across the worlds, you chase him, run from him."

I blinked. "Well, that's nice and clear-"

"He wants us all. He wants us to fall. The world to end with him only left to rule the living and the dead!"

The wind picked up before I could respond and, like smoke in shadow, they flowed away. The sighing of the spirits in the breeze sounded like a dog baying on the hunt. I shivered, feeling like the prey in this chase.

I turned to Mercy. "This is just becoming a journey of riddles and random crap, you know that?"

Mercy frowned. "Yeah. And that isn't normal."

"You didn't think to mention that before?"

She shrugged. "It's not like we get a lot of technically-still-alive people visiting in spirit form from Midgard. None of this is normal, strictly speaking."

I shivered and peered after the vanished spirits. "Well, I say this world needs to find our rear-view." I caught her querying look. "Let's leave it behind."

I gestured for her to take the lead again, and we trudged on. This time, we both looked around often, not wanting to get caught off guard again. After another long trek, we came to the frozen river. Mercy turned to follow it, and I sighed. This was the longest walk I'd been on in a while.

Since I wasn't technically physical, it wasn't exactly tiring, but I was weary from the repetition of steps and the monotonous landscape. After a while, I simply stared at the river as we walked next to it.

I barely noticed the bridge until we stopped to turn onto it. The thing was ancient and rickety, but Mercy started across it without hesitation. I watched her for a few steps, then followed, swallowing down my fears. On the other side, Mercy turned back the way we'd come from on the other side.

"Hey, Mercy, are we there yet?"

She glanced at me and rolled her eyes. "Don't start. In fact, just keep an eye out for the cave."

"Cave?"

The Valkyrie nodded. "It's somewhere around here, but the landscape changes where things are, like shifting sand dunes, so I'm not sure-"

"Is that it?" I pointed to a dark spot against a small hillock only a few yards from the river.

She sighed and glared at me. "Yes, that's it."

We hurried over to the cave opening and stepped in. A pair of torches and a flint lighter sat just where the faint light cut off. Mercy handed me a torch and quickly lit both of them.

"Let's move. This won't be pleasant, so move quickly."

I nodded and followed her through the tunnels. I noticed they were strangely familiar, but I couldn't place why until we entered a cavern lit by magical fires.

"Oh shit," I muttered, rounding the cavern wall to stare up at the monster chained there. "Hey, Fenrir. How's it going?"

CHAPTER 19

"Hello, monster," the great wolf said. "Have you come to torment me again?"

I turned to Mercy. "So this place exists both here and on Midgard?"

She nodded. "It is one of only a few places where the worlds touch each other. That's why we are here. It is a doorway between worlds and one of the only ways to get to our next destination."

I thought for a moment, not really needing the tingle of the Fourteenth Runespell or the knowledge it gave me. "Helheim."

Mercy nodded. "You did say you wanted to see all of the Nine Realms."

I sighed. "Yeah, but I forgot how many of them sucked for humans." I shook my head. "Oh well. Lead on."

Mercy walked over to the wall next to Fenrir. He watched her with his yellow-red eyes, but he didn't try to interfere. I moved to stand next to her, eyeing the wolf cautiously.

"He won't hurt you here," Mercy murmured. "He gains no advantage."

"But I have the Runespells," I whispered.

She shook her head. "The Runespells only work in Midgard."

I frowned. "Then why have I been able to use them?"

Mercy shot me a look of alarm. "What? Which ones?"

I shrugged. "The Fourteenth."

She frowned. "No others? The Fourteenth is knowledge. It puts information in your mind. You might say it works on your brain." She reached for the wall. "You and your brain are still in Midgard, really. That must be how it works."

Her hand went into the wall, and she pulled me through with her.

"I would bet the Eleventh works that way, too," she said, as if we hadn't just crossed a portal into another realm.

"Good to know," I muttered.

The room we were now in was a true underground cavern. Water dripped in the distance, distorted by the echoes. A stairway carved from the stone of the walls led up.

The Valkyrie led me to the stairs, and we began the long climb. The only thing I noticed changing was the amount of dampness on the walls. I was soon lost in the chugging rhythm of our feet and legs pushing us up the steps, inches at a time.

We had to have climbed a full mile by the time we reached the top. We paused at the top to orient ourselves. My mouth fell open.

The hall was beautiful in a stark gothic style, with arches and stained-glass windows everywhere. The tall, lean lines of the room was at odds with what I'd expected from the goddess of the realms of death.

The stained glass depicted scenes that I recognized from Norse myths. In one window, Thor wrestled Jörmungandr after catching the giant serpent while fishing in Midgard. In another, Loki, as an eagle, flew off with the fruits of immortality, stolen from Idunna. Another scene showed the chaining of Fenrir and Tyr losing his hand. The largest, central window depicted the Great Cosmic Cow, Auðumbla, licking salt off the rocks from the river, Élivágar, to reveal Búri, grandfather of Odin himself.

"Wow," I whispered.

"Yeah," Mercy agreed. She nudged me and pointed ahead of us.

The hall was not empty. People bustled all around as if in a hall or castle among the living. Some carried clothes, some bowls, and others carried trays. Mercy called one of the passing women over.

I stepped forward to look around a column, and the scene out of one of the windows came into view. It was a mountain that shined with such beauty, it nearly blinded me.

I blinked as I looked away. Mercy was at my side with a damp cloth, wiping my face.

"What-?"

"Do not look at Helgafjell without cleaning your face," she said. "You have no small gift of sight, and you are still alive. That is all that saved you this time."

"Helgafjell? The sacred mountain of the afterlife?" I nearly pushed past her to look again, but her warning held me back as much as she did. "That's the afterlife where people get to just live with their friends and family, right?"

Mercy nodded, making a few more swipes before nodding to herself. "That should do. And, yes, that is the best of all afterlives for us."

I peered around the column again. The mountain was still beautiful, but it wasn't so blinding as before. I could see people moving toward and around it.

"Why are there so many out here?" I asked.

Mercy shrugged. "The Norse are a travelling people. It wouldn't be an ideal afterlife if you never got to get out." She looked around. "Here, the people earn credit to travel to other realms for a short time. As long as they follow the rules, they get to return without a problem."

I blinked. "Huh, so Hel is quite the bargainer."

"I thought you'd understood that the last time we met, mortal."

I turned toward the voice, flinching at the sight that I knew was coming. Again, the shifting blackened, decaying corpse flesh and writhing, maggot-like regrowth turned my stomach. I swallowed hard and tried to ignore it.

"Hel," I said. "Thank you for allowing us to visit your realm."

The goddess chuckled. "So sayeth the gatecrashers. It's not like you asked for an invite first." She waved her hand at one of the people moving around. "But let it not be said I am a poor host. Drink with me."

A woman brought a tray with three goblets and a pitcher. Hel poured a measure for each of us and raised her cup. "To my guests. May they leave as healthy and intact as they have arrived."

I glanced at Mercy as she hesitantly drank. She swallowed, then nodded at me. I sipped the drink, surprised to find it a refreshing, citrusy mead.

"Very nice," I praised, holding the goblet up. I looked at the creature of death, my hostess. "You honor us." I let the implied question hang in the air.

Hel shrugged and led us to a balcony of gray granite. The mountain was the primary view, but, below us, people moved around.

"What do they all do?" I asked. "I mean, aside from the general earning of a vacay."

Hel glanced down at them as if looking at a piece of furniture. "They prepare tonight's feast." She looked up at me as one of her eyes changed from a milky cataract to a dry-blackened, sunken orb, and the other did the opposite. "You should join us."

I ignored the invitation for the moment. "Feast? For who?"

"My honored guests, the most beloved of the dead."

Mercy, standing on my other side, let out a small gasp. "Baldr."

Hel nodded. "Among others. He is always a part of the feasts, though." She sipped from her cup again, watching me with those creepy eyes over the rim. "You'd like him."

I glanced at Mercy. "Well, then. Far be it from us to miss such an opportunity." I raised my own goblet, hoping I wasn't making a mistake. "We'll be there."

CHAPTER 20

Mercy and I were shown our seats. Hel had provided us with unusual outfits – pants with calf-length skirts, and shirts with half-corsets. The material was fine wool with silk embroidery.

I felt like someone's doll, all dressed up and held together with only a few stitches. Nothing was exactly uncomfortable. It was the idea of it that was the problem.

It was what I would wear for anything other than a fancy dinner. It felt fake.

Mercy grabbed my hand. It took me a moment to realize I'd been pulling at the laces of my half-corset. It was a nervous action, but I'd be spilling out of my clothes if I kept it up.

We sat down next to the head of the table, and I folded my hands tightly in my lap. It wasn't that I was necessarily afraid of or intimidated by the people there or the people who would be there. I just had no idea what to expect, and that lack of knowledge fed my anxiety.

Mercy murmured tidbits of information as the feast progressed. She pointed out a few interesting people as they entered and sat. She let me know that the feast wouldn't properly start until the first toast, which would be led by Hel herself, as the host of the event.

I tried to remember names and faces and etiquette, but I felt distinctly overwhelmed. I sipped at my cup of mead, which was constantly checked and refilled by women carrying around giant horns filled with the drink.

The people serving and seating were both men and women, but the mead was only dispensed by the women. I asked Mercy why that was.

"Mead is the purview of women," she said.

I gave her a blank look.

"Okay, mead is served by hosts to their guests. Guests are visitors to the house, which is owned and run by women. Mead is an alcohol. Brewing takes time and darkness, so it is done by those who have a stable home and don't journey much. That is mostly women."

I nodded my understanding, and then nodded a greeting to a couple being seated across from us.

Mercy wasn't finished with the explanation, though. "Mead is made from honey, which represents the sweet bounty of the land, the healing touch of the völva, and certain aspects of sex and women."

"Oh, yes." I gestured for her to continue. "I get what you're... saying."

She nodded. "And honey is made by bees, and bees are ruled by a queen, a female."

"Right, got it," I murmured. "Mead is just girly from start to finish."

Mercy shot me an exasperated look and rolled her eyes. "The sacred drink makes rituals even more special, but sure..."

The murmur of conversations around us grew louder, and I lost myself in people-watching as the seats along the great tables filled up. I was unobtrusively studying the embroidery along the sleeve of a man sitting several chairs down from me and across the table when movement at the formal head of the table drew my attention.

I gaped at the man who, along with Hel at his side, was settling into his chair. As horribly beautiful as Hel was, this man was almost painfully gorgeous. His blond hair and beard were trimmed and groomed to a casual perfection. His blue eyes were knowing and alert, yet soft and kind.

His kilt-like clothing fit perfectly, following the lines of his muscles to enhance the quality of his form. He also wore a short, fine cape around his shoulders, leaving his chest bared. He was obviously muscular, but not overly so. There was just enough softness to his physique to make me want to touch...

"Nicola."

I jumped, staring at Hel who had a smirk on her face as she spoke. "This is Lord Baldr, my most honored guest."

I flushed and muttered something I hoped was a polite greeting.

Then he spoke. His voice was like silk and warm water, flowing over me in a way that was nearly embarrassing. "-so good to meet a quest hero. Have you met my lady wife, Nanna?"

I blinked and followed his gesture to the pale, dark-haired beauty beside him. A snowy white kerchief of fine linen held her hair in place, and she smiled lovingly at her husband before returning her gaze to me.

I looked from one to the other for a moment before speaking, drawing on the Fourteenth Runespell for knowledge. "Mistress Nanna, it honors me to look into the face of joy and the only light that can brighten the deepest night. The tales do you no justice."

I knew I'd hit the right note when both she and Baldr smiled, and Hel quirked an eyebrow while trying not to smile.

I continued, drawing the godly couple into discussion. "Do you live here in this wonderous hall, or is Breiðablik your home? I could never figure out if it was here or in Asgard."

"Technically," Mercy said. "It moved here when Baldr did, though it was more of an individual residence and- Well, I guess you might call it a temple."

I nodded. "Ah. I'd heard it was the most beautiful of halls."

Baldr and Nanna exchanged glances, and I caught an undercurrent of concern. I looked at Mercy, hoping she would know what was wrong.

She smiled at the couple. "Such a sacred place would, of course, not be ideal for hosting. Forgive us if our curiosity gave the impression that we expected such from you."

My eyes went wide when I realized what Mercy was saying. I hurried to agree. "Oh, yes, I'm not angling for an invite, really. I just want to hear about it." I cleared my throat glancing at Mercy and Hel before finishing weakly. "You know, just whatever you are comfortable sharing."

Nanna smiled while Baldr let out the most musical, masculine laugh I'd ever heard.

"You are fine, Nicola," Mercy said. "They are being a bit over sensitive. It is seen as a friendly joke among the Aesir, though why he thinks you should get it, I don't know."

I smiled at the gods, trying to show I was a good sport, even if I wasn't completely sure of what was going on.

Baldr lifted a hand, making a "calm down" motion. "You are right, Valkyrie. We should not be so mean." His voice ran over my skin in a way that was almost intimate. "Let us speak like normal, slightly uncomfortable dinner companions."

I grinned. "Sounds like a good time to me."

CHAPTER 21

I dreamed of running, of being hunted, of people calling my name to help me, to entrap me. I awoke in the land of the dead and immediately thought of the girls.

I hoped that Joseph was okay and not comatose. Surely, he would have gotten a hold of my mother by now.

I snorted at my own thoughts. As if I had a real sense of time in the spirit realms. What a ridiculous hope. It was as likely I'd been out for only 10 minutes as it was 10 months.

Mercy walked in and eyed me. "You look much more energetic. You want to get going?"

I shrugged. "Sure. Where to now?"

"I considered checking out niflhel, but we can also head over to Freyr's hall. It's not far from Tyr's, which is one of the places Fenrir's prison bridges worlds."

I nodded and bounced on the balls of my feet for a moment. "Either one is good for me."

"Let's take the horses," Mercy suggested.

The innocent tone of her voice should have warned me. But I suspected nothing until I was staring at huge steeds that were part fully living horses of every conceivable color and the dried bones of skeletal horses stripped of all flesh and skin.

The woman working in the stables brought me a steed of opalescent blue with a navy mane and one eye of blue fire while the other was perfectly equine. I mounted the simple saddle on the beast with some hesitation. The creature stomped a skeletal hoof and tossed its head, prancing in the small space.

I glared at Mercy. "Aren't they... lively?"

Mercy rolled her eyes at my pun. "Come on, hero. Show us what you're made of."

"Mostly anxiety and a crippling fear of heights," I muttered, trying to guide the creature out of the stable and onto the road behind Mercy's cotton-candy pink mount.

Once out and pointed in the right direction, the creatures promptly ignored their riders and simply raced along the road, snorting flames of green at each other. I soon found the rhythm and relaxed in the saddle.

I glanced over at Mercy, who had also relaxed into the gait. "So why do these... whatever you call them. Why do they look so... um, colorful?"

Mercy laughed. "Most horses in the spirit worlds look pretty odd in some way. I think it's because of the fascination horses hold for the children in Midgard. You might call them the foals of the human imagination."

I nodded as we came upon a grove of trees surrounding the road. The path turned dark and shadowy within the trees, and I couldn't see the other side.

Mercy dismounted, and I followed suit. "So, why are we here?"

The Valkyrie nodded at the dark copse. "Niflhel is where the worst of beings are kept after death. Even their presence would degrade the afterlives of others, so they are separated. There."

She stepped forward and I followed without hesitation. That surprised me. I was curious about the closest thing to the Christian hell that the Norse realms had, but it was still not something I necessarily wanted to experience.

We strode into the thicket and along the darkening path. Within a few moments, it was as dark as midnight. My steps slowed when I could no longer see the ground, but I kept moving forward. A sickly yellow-green glow showed several beings approaching. I glanced over at Mercy. Her expression was concerned, which somehow calmed my own reaction.

I turned to the beings and greeted them. "Thank you for allowing us to visit, spirits of the dead-"

One of the beings began laughing. It was a cruel sound, and I barely kept from flinching.

"At least, mortal, you did not call us 'honored'," he said. "That would have been a blatant lie, and nigh unforgivable. Then you would be no better than we are."

I stared the being down. His words were a little too close to Jehovah's accusation for my comfort. After a moment, I remembered a drop of wisdom that I'd picked up from popular media. "Only evil deals in absolutes," I said. "Perhaps your being unforgiving has made you unforgivable."

The being raised his eyebrows. "An interesting thought. I'll have centuries to ponder it. Thank you for that entertainment. We have travelled the world several times between us all, yet we bore each other with the same stories and arguments. Ask and we shall answer one question true."

I frowned. "Oh, um." I glanced at Mercy, but she shrugged with wide eyes.

I thought wildly, trying to come up with something. I wanted to make it count. It should be a question I really wanted answered. But I also wanted to be sure I didn't waste it, that it would give me the most information. I thought about the gods and creatures I'd already met.

Inspiration hit me. "Why should I look for Odr?"

The spirit beings recoiled. They flowed around each other, agitated, for several moments before facing me again.

"When you find Odr, many mysteries will be solved. When you discover Odr, many will become one. When you track Odr, there will be celebration and mourning for that which was lost, found and destroyed. When you catch Odr, you will stop Jehovah's plans."

I opened my mouth, but the being who spoke gestured sharply. "We have given more than you deserved. Leave now, mortal, lest we take our due in pieces of your life and feast on your memories."

My eyes went wide with shock, and I backed away. I caught a glimpse of Mercy out of the corner of my eye. She was moving back as well. After a few steps, we both turned and ran back to the mounts. Or, at least, in a direction we assumed to be back toward the beasts. I could hear a soft, amused voice calling my name over and over. It didn't quite sound like the spirits.

I stumbled once we left the sickly glow of the dishonorable dead. My feet lurched forward, hopeful each time I would reach the end of the blind darkness. Instead, I just staggered another step. I choked, hopelessness creeping through me. I was going to be trapped in this darkness forever, fleeing from beings too evil to be near the rest of the dead.

Finally, the soft glow of Helheim's twilight appeared before me. Another few steps and I spotted the mounts. Mercy was nearly brushing against me, she was so close to my side. We linked arms and staggered to the mounts, not stopping until we were in the saddles and heading back to Hel's hall.

"Why do you keep taking me to meet these... weird... things?" I demanded, rocking with the creature's gait.

Mercy shook her head. "I was told I needed to take you to meet Heidr by a völva. One of the Norns said you could die if you didn't see all of the Nine Realms, including Niflhel."

I stared at her. "And you didn't think to tell me? To warn me? Here I thought we were going on a fricken' amusement park style jaunt, and, instead, we are facing down fire giants, the evil dead, and gods know what else is waiting."

Mercy avoided my eyes. "Well, it got you to come with me. I just didn't think you would go for the truth. A jaunt is fun and exciting. I decided you needed that more than an obligatory inspection."

I shook my head. "Fine. I get it. But no more tricks and lies. I'm having enough trouble with navigating this crap without you playing god-creature games with me, too."

Mercy nodded. "Okay. That's fair." She looked over at me. "So are you ready to move on? Back to Asgard for a bit."

I nodded. "Yeah, I could use the break from this craziness."

CHAPTER 22

We said our goodbyes to Hel, Baldr and Nanna. I was a little jumpy, wondering if we might have broken some obscure rule and would have to stay in Helheim. Instead, we were shown off with as much ceremony as we'd been greeted.

We stepped into the bifrost and I let the overwhelming sensory experience wash over me. I zoned out for a moment, until something caught my attention. I jerked into alertness, reaching out with my senses and energy to try to find it. It took me a moment to catch on that the feeling was the disturbance.

It was a sense of betrayal, like some being had violated their own nature. It felt like someone had been hurt by that. There was anger and tears, and bitter, bitter vengeance growing over the years.

"Tyr. Fenrir." I reached out to the feeling and pulled it close. I popped out of the bifrost and stood in shock at the expanse of emptiness.

Before me was blackness. Not the blackness of a sealed room with no light. Not the blackness of deep space. Not the blackness of unconsciousness. Somehow, all of those were glowing with presence and life compared to this.

I drew in a ragged breath, near tears for no reason at all, except that the blackness somehow stole hope from my mind and heart. I turned back to the bifrost, convinced that the silver-blue ribbon couldn't possibly exist here.

The bifrost wound its way around a giant tree, with infinite roots reflecting its infinite branches. The tree itself was alight with the vibrant glow of fire and ice. The ice floated along the top of a giant river, while the underside of the current sparked with flames and magma.

I stared in horrified fascination as scenes along the tree stood out clearly to me. A spot within the roots, near one of three massive, main roots, suddenly jumped into focus. The Well of Urdr sat among the twisting wood, while women of all kinds moved around it, tending their work.

A thread weaving along the lowest roots grew into the monster serpent, Niðhoggr, who chewed on a mid-sized root until it was just a few ragged strands of fiber. The beast moved its head to nip at a spirit floating nearby.

I jerked away from the scene only to find myself staring at the uppermost branches. Several of the boughs resolved into the tines of the antlers of four giant bull elk. An eagle flapped down to rest on one of the tine-branches. The elk shook its head, and the eagle took off, flying around the crown of the tree several times before attempting to rest again.

A small movement showed a large brown squirrel with a thinly furred tail and black tufts on its ears. It raced over to the eagle, chittering. The raptor let out a scream before taking off around the branches again.

I knew the squirrel must be Ratatoskr, the troublemaker, taking a likely made-up message down to the serpent. When the message was delivered, the serpent growled and shifted.

That was how the heart of the Nine Worlds beat. The giant eagle shook the branches, and the giant serpent shook the roots, and that pulse kept the tree growing steadily.

I could also see Helheim, where we'd just left, along the path of the ice and fire river, Élivágar. I could see from here that the river was actually a network of waterways flowing throughout the worlds. The river flowed around the tree, coming out of and going back into the black void behind Yggdrasil.

I turned back to the void, Ginnungagap, and tried looking into it again. This time, I spied a small glimmer to one side, along Élivágar, near the Great Tree. With a thought and a shift, I sped over to the spot. On the icy side of the river network, a huge sheet of ice had formed. Within it, there was a hollow, as though there had been something within the ice that had been since freed.

Buri, I thought. The ancestor of humans and gods all had been licked out of the salty cosmic ice by the great cosmic cow. What a start for life in the Nine Realms...

But why was I here?

I thought back to the feelings I'd latched on to in the bifrost. I had thought they were about Tyr and Fenrir, but neither of them had any real connection to Ginnungagap. At least, no more than the general stuff that everyone had.

"You are one of the mortals of Midgard." The gentle voice sounded muted in the void, but it still startled me.

I turned to find myself face to face with a wide brown face. The eyes were covered with long strands of thick, woolly hair, and the long furry ears each twitched under a large tuft of even more of the thick hair. I pulled back and gaped at the black nose before refocusing on the creature as a whole.

"A-a cow!" I said. "I mean, you're a cow! Er, I mean... Um, you have to be that cow." I glanced at the heavy head that bore no horns. The Fourteenth Runespell tingled against my chest. "Auðumbla, the hornless cosmic cow, creator of the rivers of milk that fed the first beings, and licker of the salt that produced Buri."

"I am," the cow said in her calm, slow voice. "Why are you here?"

I shook my head. "I was just trying to figure that out. I was in the bifrost, and I felt what I thought was the guilt and betrayal of Tyr and Fenrir. Instead, I ended up here."

The cow nodded. "Betrayal is not unique to the wolf and the one-handed god."

I frowned. "Did something happen here? A betrayal of that magnitude?"

Auðumbla looked at me, then turned to the ice wall. She licked at it a few times. "It took three days to reveal the thing inside the ice. Before that, there had only been ice and me. I wanted another thing. I didn't know what it would be or what it would bring."

I reached out to touch the ice with my hand. It felt like ice, normal ice, melting slightly under the warmth of my fingers. I licked them and tasted the salt. It was strangely delicious, and I nearly reached out for another taste.

"I returned to the ice over and over," the cow continued. "First was the giant, Ymir, who drank of my milk while I tasted the ice. Others came from them. But not Buri. I uncovered Buri."

I nodded, entranced by the storytelling of the soft-spoken bovine who had helped create the Nine Worlds.

"Buri's son, Borr, found Bestla, and they created Odin, Vili and Ve, knowledge, will and spirit." The cow paused. "When the brothers were born, I sometimes felt like someone was feeding from me again. I thought it might be Ymir again, but it continued after the brothers killed the giant and used their body to form the Nine Worlds."

I frowned. "There was someone else?"

The creature blinked at me from under the hair covering her eyes. "I do not know. And you should not be out here. One can lose much in the void, even themselves."

I swallowed hard, cutting my eyes to the terrible but seductive darkness. It called to me, sang to me, like howling wolves.

I backed up, moving toward the bifrost. "Thank you, Auðumbla."

I turned and only looked back once, curious about the lack of response. The cow had gone back to licking the salty ice, ignoring me as though I'd ceased to exist.

CHAPTER 23

I tried focusing more on Tyr as I knew him. We'd only met a few times, but the god had left an impression. He was, for lack of a better term, admirable.

He had sacrificed more than his hand to trap Fenrir. He had also laid his reputation down, lying to the great wolf as the god of truth. It wasn't like he did it without consequence either. The guilt on his face, in his voice when he spoke of it, was obvious.

He was the first to tell me I would lose more than I'd anticipated in my quest. And he was the first I'd really believed when he told me he understood my conflict over that. After all, he'd experienced pretty much the same in his own situation.

I embraced that feeling of kinship, guilt, and sorrow. I pulled at the feeling, waiting to be spit out of the bifrost again. And I staggered down the gentle slope, knee-length grass tangling around my ankles. I caught my balance and stood upright, looking around.

At the top of the hill stood a small building, much like Valhalla, but somehow trimmed. It was like all the rougher edges had been smoothed out. The thatching didn't stick out nearly as much. The wood seemed more finished. Even the river rock used for the base of the building seemed more regularly shaped.

Coming down to meet me, Mercy strode with a familiar man. He wore jeans and a button-up shirt. His well-groomed beard was shorter than most of the Norse gods, and his hair was done in a short, modern style.

His left hand swung loosely by his side, while the sleeve of his right arm was tucked into his pocket. He walked lightly, but his eyes seemed much older than his face. The few lines on his face seemed etched in stone.

"Tyr, Mercy," I said. "Surprise, surprise, I got lost again."

Mercy shook her head. "I'm going to have to put a leash on you, if you keep this up."

I grinned. "I cannot be tamed!"

Tyr rolled his eyes. "Welcome to my home, Nicola. Welcome to the Hall of Truth."

I looked up at the longhouse. "Thank you, Tyr. You honor me with your welcome." I glanced over at Mercy. "Do we have time?"

Mercy nodded. "Of course."

Tyr led us back up to the top of the short slope. I had to admire the view of beautiful forests and a crystalline stream cutting through the valley at the base of the hill. I spotted some elk and smaller deer on neighboring slopes, watching us as we checked out the pure nature of the place.

Finally sated with the visuals, I turned to find Tyr and Mercy smiling as they watched me. I raised my eyebrows, but Tyr simply gestured for us to go to the longhouse. After a brief tour, we sat with mugs of mead and plates of sweet, scone-like biscuits filled with berries.

"Still struggling with your obligations?" Tyr asked after a short silence.

I swallowed the bite I'd been chewing, then swallowed a mouthful of mead. Just for good measure and delaying the answer, I swallowed again. Finally, I nodded. It was safer than trying to talk.

"Is your family supportive…?" His voice trailed off as I shook my head. "Dammit. That's the worst. Not having people standing by you, even when you have to stand alone."

I shrugged and took a big bite of a blueberry filled bread. I chewed, hoping the dryness in my mouth would resolve itself. Instead, all the moisture seemed to be rerouted to my eyes. I sniffed and took a swig of mead. It took a few more swallows to get all the crumbs out of my mouth and down my emotion-tight throat.

Finally, I met Tyr's eyes. There was no judgment, like I feared. It was just sorrow and understanding. I offered a shaky smile. "There's nothing to do about it. I have you guys and that'll have to do."

Tyr frowned but nodded. A short, lighthearted chat later, Mercy and I took our leave and headed across the hills toward a rocky area closer to the foot of the mountain range that was the vague backdrop of every place I'd been so far in Asgard.

We walked in silence for what seemed hours, deep in the pensive mood that our visit with Tyr had put us in. Occasionally, rabbits or squirrels would burst out of the grass or brush nearby and race away. The whole effect was a fairy tale-esque landscape.

We rounded a hill and I gasped. A wonder of natural architecture stood tall on a lush outcrop of rocky cliff. It was made of a foundational layer carved out of the rock itself. The earth-packed frame of wooden beams and branches looked like a tangle of brush and vines with mosses and ferns filling the gaps.

Even the few people milling around seemed more a part of the natural landscape. Most of them wore furs and leathers as much as woven-fiber clothing. The weapons they were working with and maintaining tended more toward clubs and bows, rather than swords and shields.

The Valkyrie headed up the steep slope with me on her heels. After a climb that left us breathless but energized, we approached the hall. A man stepped out of the door, stretched and looked around.

We stopped in our tracks, staring. The man was slightly above average in height, and well-muscled. He wore trousers and a sash across his otherwise bare chest. He had long, well-kept brown hair and a beard with twin bead-laced braids going from the corners of his mouth to join at his chin in a chevron.

I realized at some point while staring that the man was attractive but not extremely so. But he had a natural aura of what I could only describe as sexuality. He was a true force of nature, and that's what told me who he was.

"Freyr," I breathed.

Mercy nodded next to me. "Yes, he is," she said, just as breathless as I was.

I glanced at her, and she gave me a wry smile and a shrug.

"He has this effect on... everyone," she admitted.

I turned back, ready to greet the god. A woman stepped out and put an arm around Freyr's waist. Her red-blonde hair shone like rich gold, yet that was only a crown for her beauty. She was the perfect foil for the god.

Freyr smiled at the woman and put his arm around her back. The pair of them turned to face us.

"Freyr, Gerdr, forgive our intrusion," I said.

Mercy glanced at me and nodded.

The divine couple smiled. Gerdr stepped forward, holding out both hands to me. "Welcome to our home, quest hero." She took my hands, then looked over at Mercy. "Valkyrie."

"Greetings," Mercy said. "You honor us with your welcome."

The pair led us to a table with a dense rye bread and soft white cheese, and a plate full of fire-blackened sausages. A pitcher dripping with condensation held chilled mead. We sat and served ourselves up the drinks and light snack, perfect after our exertions.

Freyr and Gerdr snuggled on a bench across from Mercy and me. After a few bites, Freyr leaned forward and stared me in the eye. I swallowed, barely able to follow his words with the distraction of his sensual mouth moving in speech.

"What tales does the quest hero bring us for our hospitality?"

CHAPTER 24

Gerdr playfully slapped her husband's arm. "Regaling us with stories is not a price we demand." She glanced at me. "But we wouldn't mind a lively talk of your adventures."

I opened my mouth to tell them about those I'd already met, but a thought hit me. "I would like to start with a riddle, of sorts." I bit the end off of a sausage and let the savory juices fill my mouth for a moment. *Was everything in Freyr's realm sensual?* "In my travels around the realms, I keep running into people talking about your sister's husband," I said. I glanced at Freyr, trying to judge his reaction.

He sat back with a serious expression. "Odr? What about him?"

I shrugged. "For a god I've never met and who has very little presence in what is going on, he's been coming up a lot in conversation. At least, I'm pretty sure that he's the 'missing god' I keep hearing about."

"And you think he has something to do with why you are here?" Gerdr asked.

I frowned. "Not that, really. At least, I don't think so. More like there's a lot of people who seem to think he is important." I shrugged. "Maybe I'm just distracting myself from all the other stuff."

"Other stuff?" Freyr asked.

"Stuff about Jehovah." I rolled my shoulders. "I may be avoiding thinking about him."

"Why?" the god asked.

I grimaced. "He's kind of after me. He thinks he can use the loophole of me being in a coma to get rid of me."

Freyr and Gerdr exchanged a look. Gerdr reached out to pat my hand. "That's not great, but you are safe here."

I nodded. "Key word, here. It's travelling the bifrost and ending up in the void or popping out near Urdr's Well that worries me."

Freyr frowned. "You have so much difficulty travelling the bifrost?"

I sighed. "More like controlling my emotions, I think. I just keep… I don't know. Latching on to the wrong feelings to navigate? I don't know a lot of these places yet, so I'm going off the stories and what little I do know. It just seems to be always wrong."

"How so?" Mercy asked.

"Like, getting to Tyr's place," I explained. "I was focusing on the betrayal and guilt. I figured that was a big part of Tyr's story. Instead, I ended up having a talk with the cosmic cow." I shook my head. "That just seems like a pretty big variation. And I don't know why these emotional things keep taking me the wrong way."

"Odd," Freyr mumbled. "Why would Ginnungagap be a location of betrayal?" He looked at Gerdr. "Ymir?"

She shook her head. "The jötun see Ymir's death as a necessity. Not favorable for Odin to have done that, but not so far as a betrayal." She offered Freyr a tight smile. "They had no real relationship. There was nothing to betray. Certainly not strong enough to make betrayal a significant part of the energy of Ginnungagap or anything in that area."

I shrugged. "So maybe I'm just jumping out in the wrong spot."

Mercy shook her head. "That's not how it works. You can't jump out in the wrong spot. You have to have a location, an emotional energy, to exit. That's not hard. Getting the right one is only a bit tricky, which is why the bifrost isn't travelled by mortals lightly."

I huffed out a wry laugh. "It isn't hard to choose, but it's hard to choose the right one."

Mercy nodded.

I sighed. "So either I'm getting worse at controlling my emotions or there's something else going on." I raised both hands, palm up, to indicate scales balancing. "Either my abilities are slowly eroding..." I raised one hand, "Or I need to look for something that..." I raised the other hand, "might not be there if it's me." I threw up both hands. "How am I supposed to objectively judge that?"

Mercy shrugged while the gods looked unsure.

"And," I added. "None of this gives me any idea of how to deal with Jehovah." I leaned back. "I just wish I knew what his deal was."

"His deal?" Gerdr asked.

I nodded. "Why he wants to start the end of the world through another pantheon. Like, why doesn't he use his own pantheon? Why does he even want the world to end? You know, what's his deal?"

Freyr nodded. "That's something none of us knows. Jehovah lived peacefully with the gods until the 4th or 5th century, common era. That's around the time the Christian church split along with the Roman Empire."

"After that, he became aggressive," Mercy picked up the narrative. "He encouraged his followers to expand, conquering those who followed other gods."

"It was personal," Freyr said, poking his finger into the top of the table as he spoke.

Gerdr crossed her arms over her chest, and Freyr frowned.

"I know you think I'm just upset," the god said. "But he moved his people north. Not as much east, and west and south were almost afterthoughts. He moved north."

Freyr gestured broadly as he spoke. "Then when Haraldsson converted, the last significant population of our followers were broken or converted. And they stopped." He crossed his arms, matching his wife. "That's a pretty big coincidence, don't you think?"

Gerdr shook her head. "It isn't that it doesn't make sense, because it does. It's just that it could be only circumstantial. And what would you do about it if it was on purpose?"

Freyr scowled, dropping his arms.

"Exactly," Gerdr said. "As far as we know, there is no benefit to pursuing that line, if it truly exists in the first place."

I frowned. "Well, it would give more information about why he might be doing this." I glanced at Mercy. "Right?"

The Valkyrie shrugged. "I don't know. After he expanded north, it's hard to say if he was pushing his followers to move on to the rest of the world, or if his followers simply kept going."

"And if they were even for the same reason," I muttered. I caught the confused looks from the others. "What if Jehovah initially did go after the Norse pantheon? He gutted the followership, which was his primary goal. But then he got a taste for being the biggest fish in the pond, the most important god in all of Midgard."

Freyr nodded. "That would make sense."

Gerdr frowned at him, then turned her scowl to me. "If it is what happened. And that's a big if. There is nothing to say it is. And, yes, nothing to say it isn't either."

I nodded. "I know. This is just hypotheticals." I sighed. "So did anything else happen around the same time that Jehovah got all aggressive?"

Mercy frowned. "Well, that was the last Convening."

Freyr and Gerdr both nodded.

"Last Convening?" I asked.

The Valkyrie nodded. "The gods used to convene to talk shop and negotiate. All kinds of things that are harder to do in the closed system of a single pantheon."

"And what happened at the last Convening?" I asked.

Mercy and the divine couple all exchanged uncomfortable looks. After a moment, Mercy cleared her throat.

"The last Convening was held here in Asgard," she said. "There was a series of sporting events, and then..."

Freyr took up the narrative. "Then Baldr did his immortality trick. All great fun until..."

Realization dawned. "Until Loki tricked Hodr into killing him," I finished.

CHAPTER 25

Mercy stared down at her hands. "Everyone was so upset, we began fighting among ourselves."

Gerdr nodded. "Then Hodr was killed in revenge, and Loki was captured and tried."

"By the time we had calmed down," Freyr said. "We had managed to scare off most of the other pantheons, and probably insulting many of them, as well."

"It was not our proudest moment," Mercy admitted. "Then Odr suggested that it was all Odin's fault. He thought that Odin should have kept control of the situation, which was rather unfair."

Gerdr rolled her eyes. "Odin doesn't have that kind of power over the rest of us, and it wouldn't end well for anyone if he tried to."

Freyr nodded. "But Odin didn't like the blaming, regardless, especially on the heels of his wife's favorite son being killed. It's one thing to hold that belief. It's another to call Odin out in the middle of a disaster."

"He actually told Odr that if he wasn't going to help get Baldr out of Helheim, Odr should leave and..." Mercy trailed off, a look of shock on her face.

"What?" I demanded.

The Valkyrie stared at me wide-eyed. "He said Odr should leave and never return."

Freyr frowned. "Was that the last time he was back?"

Mercy nodded. "I think so."

I looked at each of the trio in turn. "What does that mean?"

Gerdr shook her head. "It means that, intentionally or not, Odin may have banished Freya's husband from Asgard."

"And as her brother," Freyr said slowly. "I should be stepping in to protect my sister's family from injustice."

I frowned. "So, what? You are going to go fight Odin over something he may or may not realize he'd done?" I leaned forward. "Do you people understand what communication is? Diplomacy?"

Freyr grimaced. "Yes, I should speak to him. But Freya is the one who needs to determine if Odin owes her for lost time with her love."

I thought about the history between Freya and Odin. They had often been lovers, and if Odin had banished Odr before initiating a tryst, that would be hard for him to defend. "This could end very badly."

The others nodded.

I blew out my cheeks. "Well, I guess that explains the whole thing about why I should find Odr, huh?"

Mercy shrugged. "It does fit, doesn't it? Maybe you are going to be able to prevent a disastrous consequence from that situation."

I grinned wryly. "Cool. Saving all Nine Realms, like it ain't no thing." I slapped my hands down on the table. "So should we be heading out, or stay for a while?"

Mercy turned to Freyr. "We appreciate the refreshment and the information, but we should take our leave."

Freyr nodded, raising his cup of mead in response. Gerdr smiled at us. "Thank you," she said. "We have enjoyed your company and conversation, as hard as the emotions and conclusions may be."

Mercy and I headed back toward the bifrost. I shook my head. "How the hell am I supposed to do this?" I demanded. "I don't even know where to begin."

Mercy shrugged. "I don't know," she admitted. "This is not what I expected for you, I promise." She shot me a look. "I might have let you out of being a quest hero if I had. This is more of a lifelong epic quest, and that's not meant to go to one with a family."

I snorted. "Me having a family hasn't been a consideration from day one."

The Valkyrie shook her head. "Actually, it has. If you weren't the hero we need-"

"Instead of the hero you deserve?" I suggested with an evil grin.

She snorted. "Okay, batman."

I laughed. "I am the minor fright that flaps in the dusk!"

"That's not right," Mercy muttered. "You are definitely not right."

The bifrost came into view, and I touched her arm to get her attention. "Seriously, though. Where are we going now?"

"I guess we should see if we can find Odr."

"And how do we do that?" I gestured to the bifrost. "Take that and hope we stumble upon the right feeling to reach him? I mean, doesn't Freya spend a lot of time looking for him? And she's got the time, the emotional connection, and the power."

Mercy shook her head. "I don't know."

"Who would?" I demanded. "We keep getting these stupid little hints and clues. Who would have more information? Who, aside from Freya, knows about Odr and where he might go?"

Mercy pressed her lips together, and I knew she had thought of something. I stared at her until she spoke.

"Some god creatures spend their whole lives travelling the Nine Realms. Some are just looking at the world, but some seek out... other things." She winced and shot me a look. "Unsavory things. Taboos in any of the realms. Sometimes horrific, sometimes just shady."

"Who does that?" I asked quietly. "Which god creature?"

Mercy shook her head. "It's dangerous. I wasn't going to take you there on your worlds tour. And those most likely to know are... not friendly. More than the others."

"Who?" I demanded.

"We have to go to Jötunheim and question the jötun," she admitted.

I took a deep breath. "Which one?"

She shrugged. "Let's see. The ones who liked to find secrets? Loki, Grýla, Vafþrúðnir. We should also talk to a few with children or grandchildren who are part Aesir or Vanir or Dwarf or Elf or even mortal."

I sighed again. "How many?"

Mercy grimaced. "Lots."

I nodded. "Who should we start with?"

"The easiest to find will be Loki," she said. "He is bound in a cave."

"Like Fenrir," I murmured. Something tickled my mind, but I focused on the task at hand. "Okay, let's go check out the boogie man."

Mercy frowned. "This isn't going to be easy. Sigyn will be there. She is very protective."

I cracked my neck. "Sounds par for the course." I caught her expression. "If I'm all scared and shaking, will it change what needs to be done?"

"No."

"Then let me have my bravado," I gritted out, holding out my hand for her to take before we entered the bifrost again. "It's about all I have right now."

Mercy squeezed my hand briefly before taking a step toward the bifrost. As we entered, I heard her say, "You have me, my friend."

CHAPTER 26

I frowned as we stepped out of the bifrost and took several steps across the glen. There were trees surrounding the small grassy space, and fluffy white clouds moved steadily across the bright blue sky above us.

I glanced at Mercy, thinking she would tell me we were in the wrong spot, but she was already striding toward a deer path in the trees across from us. I hurried after her, looking around as I did.

I noticed the plants were all hardy looking. There were no delicate flowers or vines to be seen. Even the moss seemed to be almost like astroturf. There were few animals moving through the foliage as we pushed through the brush that had grown across the path.

Between one step and the next, the climate changed. The late summer sun was immediately blocked by a frigid, blinding white blizzard. I stumbled as the calf-deep snow appeared almost under my feet. With the wind howling in my ears, I couldn't talk to Mercy. Instead, I struggled on, moving forward in the Valkyrie's tracks. I wondered if freezing to death was possible as an astral spirit.

A few yards after the snow began, the falling flakes disappeared in a sweltering heat. The sun appeared again, twice the size and ten times as hot. The shivering that shook my whole spine was still slowing when the sweat began running into my eyes and down my back.

"What is this place?" I asked, gasping as the heat stole the moisture from my throat. "It's like weather ADHD."

Mercy shot me a wry look. "The jötun are forces of primal energy. Weather energy. They rule this land, and the weather reflects that."

"It was nice where we landed," I grumbled.

"Only when we landed there," she corrected. "I'm sure it's changed by now."

I shook my head. The deep snow was gone, but the heat was just as effective in slowing my steps to a crawl. I considered pestering Mercy with more questions, but the extreme temperatures stole my ambition.

It seemed another eternity before the weather changed again, this time to a driving wind. I held up my hand to block the leaves and branches that flew toward my face. I leaned into the wind, staggering against it.

When the wind quit, I stumbled forward several steps, nearly falling into a river that had seemingly appeared before us.

I looked around, finding the scene to be much the same as the glen we'd come into. The major difference was the high cliff upstream. The top of the cliff had a heavy mist flowing over the edge and a cascading waterfall where the river and cliff met.

Mercy was already making her way around the mossy wet rocks along the bank. I caught up to her just as she reached a path meandering along the edge of the cliff. It disappeared behind the waterfall.

"That's where Loki is?" I asked.

"Yup." The Valkyrie stepped on to the path. "Careful, though. There's earthquakes, and it's quite a fall from the top."

I nodded, watching my footing cautiously. The earthquakes were Loki, raging as poison dripped into his eyes for the few seconds his wife, Sigyn, stepped away to dump the bowl she caught most of the poison in. It was his part of the punishment for Baldr's death.

We were just over halfway up when I felt the ground start to rumble under my feet. I clung to the rocky wall as the shaking grew worse. My hand found a root arching out of the dirt, and I grabbed it, hoping it was strong enough to hold me. A moment later, the shaking calmed. Mercy and I leaned against the wall, catching our breath.

"That was intense," I muttered.

Mercy laughed. "Yeah, it is. That's why he doesn't get many visitors."

I grinned as we continued on, the weather changing to a mild, gray drizzle. The rocks under our feet became slippery with algae and water as we moved under the edges of the waterfall itself. After a tense few yards, a large outcrop appeared, blocking the spray from falling directly onto us. Another few feet, and the outcrop widened into the mouth of a cave.

The space was surprisingly dry and well-lit only a few feet inside. The temperature was cozy and almost homey. We moved farther into the cave until we came upon a tunnel. There was a space nearby that was covered with a large hide, like a curtain.

Mercy noticed me looking at the hide. "Guest quarters," she said. "For visitors."

I raised an eyebrow, and she shrugged.

"They are almost never used."

I nodded as we headed down the narrower tunnel. There were no light sources in the cave or the tunnels, but the light was a constant ambient glow, as if the air itself was providing the soft illumination.

It took a moment for me to recognize the sound of a soft voice over the white noise of echoes of the water falling outside and of our scuffing footsteps. Once I heard it, though, my mind latched on to the sound, straining to decipher the words. It slowly resolved into a pair of voices, one soft and higher pitched, the other lower and with a bitter bite to it.

The tunnel curved around and then opened up into a larger cavern. Before I could get clear of the tunnel wall and Mercy's back to see in, the rumbling of the earth began again beneath my feet. I could hear the clank of metal as the floor heaved and shuddered, throwing me against the tunnel wall and onto the ground. Dirt fell around me, dusting us in a grayish tan film.

Mercy helped me to my feet, and we turned to enter the cavern, brushing dust off ourselves absently. The obvious feature was the huge platform in the center of the space. It was the size of a twin bed, though the granite of white speckled with black didn't look comfortable.

A strange leathery rope held arms and legs in place at the wrists and ankles. Another rope immobilized the neck, while two others crossed over the body, preventing any movement much more extensive than the thrashing and shifting which caused the earthquake.

I focused on the body itself. The mostly naked male form was lean and graceful, slithering within its bonds. The slender, beardless face was not masculine. Nor were the hands and feet masculine. In fact, only the absence of breasts indicated that the form was male.

The copper hair was no help either, falling in soft, shiny waves that could have been a woman's hair as easily as a man's. The texture, style and even where it was on the body gave no hint as to masculinity or femininity. Overall, the effect was that this being was perfectly agender.

I was suddenly afraid of the trapped form. "Loki."

CHAPTER 27

Next to Loki's prone form, a slender blonde woman sat on a boulder. She looked exhausted and bored, holding a bowl almost as large as she over Loki's face. A steady dripping sound came from the bowl, barely audible over the sound of the two jötun murmuring to each other.

Sigyn sounded like she was trying to calm Loki for the millionth time. Loki's voice was the bitter tone I'd heard earlier.

I looked above the pair and gasped at what was on the ceiling of the chamber. There was a tangle of what looked like metal roots and serpentine flesh. The roots tied around the snake, pinning it in place.

One root twined between the jaws of the serpent, holding its mouth open in place over Loki's head. The snake shifted constantly, and the movement caused the root in its mouth to milk the venom from its fangs in a steady drip.

I realized the leathery ropes must be the intestines of Loki's son, Narfi. I swallowed hard. The gods had not been forgiving after Baldr's death. I wondered for a moment how frightening the battle-ready Norse gods had been to the other pantheons.

Other gods from around the world were just as bloodthirsty, I knew. It was a coin toss as to whether this was truly horrific on the deity scale of terrors.

"-have visitors."

Sigyn's comment drew my attention back to her and Loki. Mercy gestured for me to follow her as she approached the pair.

"Greetings, Sigyn." She nodded to the goddess, then turned to Loki, crossing her arms over her chest. "Hello, Trickster. We have questions for you."

The glaring eyes were red and swollen from the venom. But they showed a level of intelligence that belied centuries of torment. "Pay the price and ask your questions."

I glanced at Mercy. "Price?"

She nodded without looking at me and waved her hands in front of her chest. With a tiny pop, a large mead horn appeared. She set it on the rock, balancing it so it would stay upright.

"A horn of mead to refresh you and your wife," Mercy said. "And my hands to hold the bowl for the time we are here, that the Lady Sigyn might be relieved of her burden for a time."

Loki's baleful eyes shifted to the woman at his side for a moment, and I could see the glare soften. "Agreed," he said. "Sit, take up your burden, Valkyrie. Quest hero, ask your questions."

Mercy took the bowl from the goddess and held it awkwardly until Sigyn had moved from her seat. The Valkyrie sat, propping her arms up the same way Sigyn had done. When she got settled, she looked at me.

"You're up, Nicola."

I shifted, feeling put on the spot. After an uncomfortable moment, I stepped closer and sat on another boulder nearby. From there, I could see Loki's eyes under the bowl. He was staring at me expectantly.

"I don't really know where to start," I said. "So I'm just going to ramble for a moment."

Amusement filled those reddened eyes as I started speaking.

"There's a chance Odin unintentionally banished Odr. That would be bad for many reasons. But we don't know for sure. What we do know is that Odr is missing, Jehovah may or may not be after the Norse gods in particular, and me specifically, and all of this is just the thing keeping me busy while I'm in a coma from being poisoned."

I stopped and took several deep breaths. "I guess the first question is the least important one. Do you know where Odr is?"

Loki smiled, though the expression still had a lot of pain in it. "I do not."

I frowned. "Do you know who does?"

"No."

"Do you have any idea where he might have been?"

"No."

I pursed my lips. A feeling of tension crawled across my shoulders, and I tried following the energy of it. After a moment, I realized my questions were close to something. The tension was Loki's expectation.

I thought my next question through carefully before asking it. "Do you know any god or god creature who knows where Odr might have been at any time after he left Asgard last?"

"I do."

"Who?"

"Garmr," he said with a smile I didn't trust. "The guard dog knows something."

"Anyone else?"

"Clarify the question." The trickster jötun smiled.

I knew he had an answer for me, but he wouldn't give it to me unless I asked a specific enough question. My last query had been too vague. There were too many ways to interpret it. So, fae-like, he refused to assume that my question meant what it would need to mean for him to give up the information.

"Do you know another god or god creature who knows the past or present whereabouts of Odr since he left Asgard?"

"No."

I frowned. "Any god or god creature who might know?"

"Yes. The ravens might know."

"Huginn and Muninn?" I shook my head. "They would have said..." I trailed off as I recounted my journey in my mind. "Except I wasn't looking for Odr when I saw them last."

I considered the information for a long moment. Then I noticed the feeling of tension again. I shot Loki a suspicious look.

"Do you know any more gods or god creatures that might know?"

"Not of any real likelihood," he said.

I shifted on the boulder. If he didn't know any others, why was there still an air of expectation around that line of questioning? I'd asked about who knew, who had known, and who might know. He said he didn't know any other-

I sat up straight. "Do you know any mortals who might know where Odr is or has been since leaving Asgard?"

The trickster laughed. "Yes."

"Who?" I felt a growing nervousness. Something about his expression made me very anxious about the answer he was about to give me.

"You."

CHAPTER 28

"Me?" I scowled at him. "What kind of game is this? I don't know where Odr is. I wouldn't know him if he was standing in front of me-Oh!" Realization hit me hard. "Do I know Odr and not know that it's him?"

Loki shifted, and I got the impression he was trying to shrug despite his bonds. "Perhaps. Perhaps not. I don't know for sure."

I scowled. "Then why would you say I know where he is?"

The trickster god's head tilted slightly to one side. He studied me for a long moment before answering. "You have twice gained information that you do not fully access. You have the Fourteenth Runespell at your neck. The sheer amount of knowledge available to you means that, statistically, you have some idea where the missing god is."

I facepalmed. "Oh gods. I forgot about all that." I looked over at Mercy, who was watching me. "The water from Urdr's Well. Why didn't I think to examine those memories for clues?"

I shook my head. "Okay, then. Next topic, I guess. Jehovah. Is he out to get any of the Norse gods?"

"Probably," Loki said. "I don't know for sure."

"Do you have any clues, indications or evidence that he is?"

"Yes. You have, I assume, spoken to Freyr. I know that he may be right. Jehovah did maneuver his followers into Norse territory over other pantheons on several occasions. Whether it was because it was

Norse territory or some obscure tactic that drove him to do so... That I don't know."

I sighed. "Well, I suppose this may be a foolish question, but... Is Jehovah after me in any part because I am a quest hero for the Norse in particular?"

"Yes."

"Why is that? What's his issue with me working for the Norse?"

"My answer is speculation only. I am not privy to his motives in specific." Loki's eyes shifted to Mercy, then the bowl. "It is time, is it not?"

The Valkyrie nodded. "I assume it goes into this hole in the corner?"

At the trickster's nod, she took a breath and met my eyes. I braced myself as she removed the bowl.

The roar as the first drops hit Loki's eyes was deafening. His body thrashed within the bonds of his own son's viscera, and the platform shook so hard, the entire cliff shuddered. I stumbled, trying to keep from being thrown to the ground. I hit the boulder I'd been sitting on with my foot, painful shocks running through my leg and up my spine.

Finally, the shaking earth calmed, and I looked up to find Loki and Mercy back in their places. Loki's eyes were redder than before. That didn't keep him from staring at me as intently as before.

I settled myself down on the boulder again and cleared my throat. "You were saying?"

The god smiled, bitter humor filling his eyes. "I was saying. Jehovah seems to be jealous of one or more of the gods of Asgard. I am... familiar with the signs of jealousy."

I nodded. Several of Loki's stories were based on jealousy, whether his or the others involved. It was odd, when I thought about it. Loki was not short on confidence, one of the sources of his many misadventures.

"You don't know who he might be jealous of though?"

"No. It does seem to be someone in Asgard, if I had to place bets."

I sighed. "That's not as helpful as I would have liked." I looked at Mercy. "Any ideas?"

She shook her head. "I'm sorry I'm not more help."

I shrugged and turned back to the trickster god, taking the time to think. "I just don't know. We have a few leads on Odr, and a tiny bit more information on Jehovah. What am I missing?"

Loki frowned, his eyes flicking up to the bowl above his face before returning to meet my eyes. "I feel I shouldn't point out the obvious if you are going to ignore it…"

I stared at the bowl. A drop landed in it with a tiny plink of sound. I followed the path of the drop to the fangs of the serpent entangled for centuries in a prison just to torture the jötun.

I looked back at his red eyes. "Venom. Poison. Yes." I took a deep breath. "I guess I have been avoiding this for… way too long."

I saw Mercy nodding out of the corner of my eye. Loki's eyes never left my face.

"Fine. Can you tell me anything about the poison that put me in a coma?"

The god smiled and it made my skin crawl. "Yes."

I waited for him to continue, but he just watched me. "I guess that was too vague for you, huh?"

"Of course." He grinned humorlessly.

"Okay. Do you know who poisoned us?"

"Yes."

"Alright. Well, paraquat poisoning doesn't usually result in a coma. Was there something mixed in with the paraquat?"

"Only the medium of consumption."

I frowned. "The spice cake. Does that mean Joseph was not poisoned?"

"Yes."

I narrowed my eyes. "How do you know about this stuff, seeing as you are bound here?"

Loki smiled. "I have my ways of keeping up with the Nine Realms, even here. And I find you interesting, so what happens to you finds its way to me."

I shifted uncomfortably. "Great," I muttered. "Another godly stalker."

The trickster just grinned at me with his red eyes. It was a look that made me feel deeply anxious.

I shifted in my seat. "So was the coma caused by the paraquat?"

"No."

I nodded. "What did cause the coma?"

"Poison."

"What?" I frowned. "So the paraquat did cause the coma?"

"No." Loki's eye glimmered with malicious humor.

I threw my hands up. "I don't get it. Am I phrasing it wrong?"

"No."

"So the coma was caused by the poison. But the paraquat didn't cause the coma. How does that–" I nearly choked on the realization. "Wait a minute. Is there more than one poison involved?"

"Yes."

My eyes widened. "No wonder the hospital was having trouble. Poisons are hard enough to identify and treat. If you stack them, it gets really hairy really quickly."

I glared at Loki, who was chuckling. I knew he was amused by the ease in which I fell into the circular thinking based on a core assumption. I was a little annoyed at myself for the same reason.

I took a deep breath. No use blaming a god of mischief. Tricksters gonna trickster. "Okay, so, two poisons. Were both intentional?"

"Yes."

"And done by the same person or group?"

"Yes."

"And what kind of poison is the other?"

"Much like the mistletoe," Loki said, his grin twisting into a snarl. "It is but a single plant in all the realms."

I frowned at him. "Which plant?"

The god wrinkled his nose. "Adelfa."

"Hm, I hadn't heard of that one." I frowned. "Why were we poisoned?"

"The water is poisoned, so the earth is poisoned. The poison earth punishes those who poison the water."

A movement at the mouth of the cave drew my attention. Sigyn had returned.

Loki's eyes went to his wife, and he laughed. "Time is up, quest hero. Quite a collection of queries have been answered. Do you feel like you know more now?"

I snorted, knowing his goal had not been to give me easy knowledge. "Only in the manner of madmen and prophets, Bound One. I thank you for your answers, regardless."

"Run, little fox," the trickster god whispered, almost to himself. "Run or be hunted."

I stood, staring at him and trembling. After a moment, I turned and gave the goddess a small bow as she passed me.

She nodded acknowledgement, then peered into the bowl and exchanged a look with Mercy. I braced myself as the Valkyrie removed and emptied the bowl once more, handing it to Sigyn.

The goddess replaced it, murmuring softly to her husband to calm him.

Mercy made her way to where I stood in the tunnel opening. We both looked back at the trio – the god, the goddess, and the serpent – before leaving without another word.

CHAPTER 29

We climbed back down the rocky path along the cliff face in silence. The mist that survived to the bottom of the cliff roiled lightly around our ankles.

"Where to now?" I asked Mercy.

The Valkyrie gave me an even look. "You are the quest hero. It is your choice what to do with the information you've been given."

I nodded. "Off to search out the ravens, then, I guess."

We struggled through the various harsh weather back to the bifrost. I nearly missed it through the pouring rain battering the once-pleasant glen.

Mercy grabbed my hand. "You take the lead this time," she shouted over the noise.

I took a deep breath, thinking of the feathered twins who had become such good friends over the years. I pulled Mercy behind me into the bifrost. I was familiar with Huginn and Muninn, so I felt confident when I found their emotional signature and stepped out of the silver-blue ribbon.

I was less sure when I checked our surroundings. It was not the astral plane, but it was very close in how it appeared. It looked like every fantasy painting of summer had merged into a single world. And I had a sneaking suspicion as to why that was.

Mercy rolled her shoulders beside me. "This is unexpected. Do you know where we are?"

I sighed as a unicorn pranced across a meadow of pink that looked like flowers. However, when the creature stepped near the blooms, they fluttered and took off as a cloud of butterflies.

"I think this is the home of the Seelie Court, the Realm of Summer," I said. I couldn't keep the defeated tone out of my voice.

Mercy seemed to immediately understand my distress. "Shit." She drew out the knife she kept in her belt at the small of her back. She examined the blade then looked at me. "Steel. Close enough to iron for our needs, I think." She sighed. "I hate Álfheimr. They are so... uptight and vicious."

I nodded. "I can't just call for the ravens here. I'd just as likely create an illusion or summon a shapeshifter or two. So we have to look the old-fashioned way."

Mercy nodded in agreement.

"Alright, boys. Where are you?" I scanned the horizon but saw nothing that might indicate the right path. Finally shrugging, we simply picked a direction and started walking.

We hiked across the butterfly meadow and turned onto a path through the woods. I swallowed my fears about fae and forests, hoping we could deal with whatever we found.

The woods got thicker and darker, and my shoulders became more tense. I started jumping whenever Mercy or I stepped on something that snapped or crackled.

"Gods, this is nerve-wracking," I muttered. "If something is going to happen, I wish it just would alrea-"

A huge shape crashed through the brush onto the path before us. I flinched, falling back. All I could make out was a flash of blue and silver before my head hit the dirt.

I lay still for a moment, my eyes scrunched shut, half convinced we were dead. Nothing else happened, except I caught my breath. Finally, I opened my eyes.

I was staring into a pale blue sky between the leaves of the trees around us. I lifted my head.

Mercy was picking herself up beside me, a scowl on her face. "That was a low blow, Frilla," she said. "Bad form."

I rolled onto my knees and began to stand. I found myself staring down the length of a silver and rose-gold spiral horn. The beast at the end of it was covered in a pale blue velvet coat. The equine face was too sharp and the eyes too intelligent.

I slowly stood the rest of the way. The unicorn kept her horn pointed in my direction as I did. I stepped back with my hands held out, trying to look non-threatening. The creature was much larger than a horse, but her body was shaped more delicately, like a deer. She had delicate hooves, though they were a single piece, like a horse's, not split like a deer's.

Her lavender mane was lush and thick, as were the lashes around her shockingly green eyes. Her tail, however, was like a zebra's with only a tuft of longer hair at the end. It was much too long, though, nearly as long as her body.

I cleared my throat. "Um, hi." I glanced at Mercy then back to the unicorn. "How are you this fine day? I hope we weren't intruding."

Mercy shook her head and chuckled. "Frilla, you are freaking my quest hero out."

"Quest hero?" The beast's voice was like a wind instrument, airy and musical.

And it came from the horn, not the mouth.

I felt my mouth fall open, but I couldn't stop gaping. Everyone knew about unicorns, but the reality, such as it was, was nothing like the cartoons back home. Even the old medieval tapestries had only touched on the truth.

The creature moved, poking me in the shoulder with her horn. It was sharp, but she wasn't trying to hurt me.

"Ouch," I said.

"You are a quest hero?" The beast's eyes moved to Mercy. "You are sure of this?"

The Valkyrie laughed. "It's her first time seeing a unicorn, Frilla. Give her a moment to get over how gorgeous you are."

The unicorn immediately began preening, arching her neck and prancing a few steps. "I am, aren't I. No wonder the quest hero is struck dumb."

I blinked. "Hey, now. I'm okay. You just need to keep a lid on..." I gestured to the creature, "all that."

The unicorn snorted, obviously pleased. "I cannot be contained, mortal. If you cannot handle all..." she pranced around some more, "this, avert your mortal eyes."

I grinned, still feeling just the slightest bit dumbstruck. "It is my greatest honor, horned one, to meet you. I am Nicola, quest hero of the Norse gods."

The unicorn tossed her mane. "Well spoke. I am Frilla, and these are my woods."

I glanced at Mercy. "Were we intruding?"

"No," the Valkyrie said. "Frilla just likes to swing her horn around with new visitors."

The beast snorted and tossed her head again. "Well, then, see if I help you."

Mercy rolled her eyes. "As if a fae creature such as you would help without a pound of flesh. Besides," she turned to brush a leaf off my shoulder. With her back to the unicorn, she winked at me. "Besides, you've likely been admiring your reflection in some still pond you've got hidden away. You wouldn't know where the ravens are anyway."

"Shows what you know, god creature," Frilla trilled. "I saw those nosy birds chatting with each other in the great oak not a few moments before I spotted you."

Mercy spun on her heel. "Really? The great oak... that way?" She pointed into the woods.

When the unicorn simply snorted again, Mercy grinned at me and headed into the woods. I glanced at the unicorn.

"You tricked me," she said, shaking her mane in anger. "How could you take advantage so?"

I blinked. "Me? Talk to Mercy. I did nothing but witness it all."

At the word 'witness', the beast's eyes narrowed. Fae hated people seeing their mistakes more than they hated people tricking them. But the offense wasn't enough for action.

I hesitated another moment before following Mercy. "I won't say a word," I promised. "Unless I must."

With the implication hanging in the still air between us, I strode into the underbrush. It took a few minutes to catch up to Mercy.

CHAPTER 30

"Do you know where we are going?" I asked.

She pointed up. I followed the gesture. There was a tree standing taller than the others. The distinct shape of the leaves told me it was an oak.

I nodded and followed her in silence. We soon came to the massive trunk of the oak. I knew it was huge, but after the massive size of Yggdrasil up close, it simply didn't compare. There in the branches of the great oak, two black shapes fluttered noisily.

I couldn't help but smile at the sight of them. "Huginn! Muninn! Hey!"

"Nicola!" The two cried as they flapped down to the soft grass under the tree's branches.

Mercy and I barely paused before flopping down beside them.

"You are here," Muninn said, flapping his wings.

"Both here," Huginn echoed.

"Yeah, I need to ask you something." I looked at Mercy. She gestured for me to continue. "It's about Freya's husband, Odr. Do you know where he is? Have you seen him at all since the last Convening of the gods?"

The ravens exchanged a look.

"We have," Huginn croaked, finally.

I waited for more, but the two stayed silent. I got the feeling they didn't want to admit what they'd seen for some reason.

"Why don't you want to talk about it?" I asked, deciding on the most direct attack.

Muninn looked at Mercy.

The Valkyrie cleared her throat. "We suspect that Odin may have banished Odr. We don't know for sure, or if it was intentional if he did. We aren't trying to start anything along those lines."

I nodded. "Heidr told me finding Odr would stop Jehovah. It's important, guys."

The ravens exchanged another look.

"Banished he was," Huginn said.

"Banish he is," Muninn agreed. "Into the desert."

"He journeyed across the sand." Huginn pecked at a spot on the ground.

"In Midgard?" I asked. "Or in one of the other realms?"

"Both." The ravens croaked the response at the same time.

"The land of the quest hero and king," Muninn said.

Huginn spoke immediately. "The land of Enmerkar."

I frowned. "Enmerkar?" I reached for the Fourteenth Runespell, hoping for the answer. The knowledge burst into my mind. "Sumerian. The middle east."

I exchanged a look with Mercy before turning back to the ravens. "Then what happened to him?"

Huginn hid his head under a wing. Muninn cawed several times before answering. "Lost him."

Huginn lifted his head. "Couldn't find him."

Both birds hopped closer to me and spoke in as close to a whisper as their corvid caws could get.

"Tell no one," Huginn croaked.

Muninn bobbed his head in agreement. "It is shame."

I smiled. "I wouldn't dream of embarrassing you by telling anyone." I looked at Mercy.

She shook her head. "Not a word. No one needs to know."

The ravens both shook their wings and hopped back and forth.

"One more thing," Huginn said.

Muninn nodded. "Two more."

I frowned, "What is it?"

"The lands of the under."

"The lands of the dwarves."

"Lives one who travels."

"Sviðr, the missing."

"Who travelled Midgard."

"The desert lands."

"He may know."

"If you can find him."

"The missing one."

"Sviðr," I said. "I will look for him. Thank you."

"And..." Huginn said.

Muninn jumped in. "Another thing."

"Thought and memory."

"Memory and thought."

"Not only names."

"Purpose, meaning."

"Remember for us."

"Think for us."

I frowned. "I-I'm not sure what-"

"The gift we gave..."

"Has more meaning..."

"Than what you've had..."

"Already. Before."

"Meaning," Huginn said, before taking off.

Muninn looked me in the eye as he extended his wings. "Not just names." He followed his twin.

I watched them until they were just two tiny dots in the sky. Then the sky swallowed them.

"That was odd," I muttered.

Mercy nodded. "But it sounds like we are off to Svartálfar, land of the dwarves."

I nodded and followed her back toward the bifrost. I looked back at the forest as we left. Frilla stood tossing her head and watching us. I got the feeling that visiting this grove again would not be as pleasant an experience for either me or Mercy.

I sighed. The Valkyrie was using up a lot of credit to help me. I only hoped it would be worth it. As we prepared to enter the bifrost once again, I heard a soft sound on the breeze. My blood froze. It was the baying of a hound. And the barking sounded too much like my name.

We stepped into a bustling street with dozens of beings. Each had skin the color of shadows in a cave, and the tallest of them stood only five and a half feet. They had no hair on their heads while each one sported beards of oily wire up to three feet long. They all wore leather aprons and pants, and shirts that looked like moss.

I stared for a moment, letting the beings shove past me on the narrow path. The stone buildings were two or more stories each and crowded together. The bottom floor had no walls, only a packed dirt floor and carved-out support beams for the floor above.

Several of the open spaces had an obvious purpose. One held a series of stalls for dark, aggressive looking ponies with no hair and flashing eyes. Another had fires burning hot with thick metal pots hanging over them. The sound of blacksmiths hammering rang out, and I could smell baking bread and scorched iron.

I lifted my gaze to the upper floors, all plain with evenly spaced windows. Every other window had a stone window box carved from the same rock as the window with various mushrooms flowing over the top and sides. Above the buildings, a flickering red lighting barely began to lighten the black stone of the sky.

Mercy pulled me to the side. I glanced at her, and she grimaced.

"The dark ones will simply get more aggressive if we remain in their way," she said. "They are an incredibly focused people."

I watched the beings passing by. There was almost a pattern to the way they shifted around each other. Some broke off from the flow to enter the shops and workshops of the buildings. Others came out of the cave-like spaces, joining the flow of people without missing a step.

"What-?" I cut myself off, not sure what I was wanting to ask.

Mercy glanced at me. "This is Svartalfheim, the land of the dark elves, sometimes called dwarves."

I nodded. "I didn't expect..." I gestured to the buildings. "We've never come out in a population center before."

The Valkyrie shrugged. "Svartalfheim is nothing but a city. They live underground in this place, carved from the rock itself. There is no way to come here without being in the city."

I noticed that the tallest buildings melded into the ceiling. I frowned, staring up at the suddenly claustrophobia-inducing stone dome that was the sky. I swallowed hard. "Underground from where?"

"We don't know," Mercy said. "Most believe it is the same world as Álfheimr, the world of the bright ones, the light elves or fae. But there doesn't seem to be a direct path between them."

I shook my head, still processing this new world. "Well, I guess we should find this Sviðr." I looked at the milling crowd of dark elves. "Should we ask for directions?"

Mercy shook her head. "They wouldn't tell us," she said. "It isn't their job. We have to go to the Directory."

CHAPTER 31

I gave her a look as she pulled me into the inexorable stream of people. Her pale skin and hair seemed to glow within the background of shadow and firelight, making her easy to keep up with.

After a short walk at an awkward but unalterable pace, we maneuvered to the edge of the stream and stepped out of it into a space with only a stone desk and two chairs. The desk was more like a counter, and the dwarf behind it watched us without change in expression.

Mercy stepped up to the desk. "Directory?"

The dark creature nodded once.

She glanced at me. "We are looking for Sviðr. Please direct us to his workshop."

The dwarf took out a large leather sheet with a grid on it. Looking closer, I saw that it was a map of the city. The Directory pointed to a spot near the center of the map.

"Your current location is here," he said, his voice like gravel crunching under tires.

He pointed to a location on the edge of the map. "The place you seek is here," he said. "You will exit this studio and turn right." He traced the path as he spoke. "Follow the stream until you reach the third intersection. Take a left and walk to the first intersection. Turn right and walk past seven studios. It will be on your right."

I blinked. "Right, third, left, first, right, seven, right?"

"Correct," he said, putting the map away. The Directory folded his hands, as expressionless as he had been when we entered.

Mercy pulled a bit of cheese out of her pocket. She unwrapped it and set it on the smooth section of stone on the desk. Then she turned to me. "Alright, let's go."

I muttered the directions under my breath as we flowed along the unrelenting current of the crowd. We nearly missed the turn-off to go left when we were surprised that the intersections worked like roundabouts. I had to push in front of a dwarf who scowled at me but barely slowed.

Finally, we were counting the studios as we passed them. "Five," Mercy muttered. "Six. Seven. Go!"

My fingers had been pressing into my leg to count off the buildings, but I had to fling my arms out to balance as we nearly leapt out of the foot traffic, which apparently got more aggressive toward the edges of the city.

The creature in the studio watched with as little expression as the Directory had. We took a moment to catch our breath before looking around. He simply watched us and waited.

The studio appeared to be set up for some kind of jeweler. I noticed a small bag full of gem encrusted torcs sitting on what appeared to be a workbench. Tools were neatly arranged along the space, lined up on the counters or hanging from hooks along the side of the tables and support beams.

"Are you Sviðr?" I asked.

"Yes," the dwarf said, his expression finally changing to caution. "You seek my skills?"

"No, we seek information you may have," I said, sitting on one of the stone pillar seats scattered throughout the studio.

Sviðr frowned, crossing his arms as he perched on his own seat. "Skill or information, both will cost you."

Mercy pulled a piece of amber from her pocket. The quail-egg sized chunk immediately drew the dwarf's attention. He took it, looking it over for several minutes before nodding and putting it into a cubby hole behind him.

"Very well, ask away."

I nodded. "About 15 centuries ago, by Midgard time, a god disappeared."

The dark creature lifted a sooty brow but remained silent.

"He may have been spotted in the lands of the Sumerian gods, of Enki and Utu. We must find him."

The dwarf pulled out an obsidian pipe and a bag. He took his time, filling the pipe with what looked like moss, then taking a hot iron rod from the fire to touch against the dried clump. He puffed at it until the clump glowed with embers, blowing the smoke out of the side of his mouth.

Finally, he pulled the black pipe from his mouth. "You speak of Odr." He glanced at Mercy then back to me. "There is danger in speaking of him and where he is."

I nodded. "Because accusing Odin of banishing Odr would lead to many troubles. We understand that. We don't care why he left or why he stayed away. We only want to find him."

Sviðr puffed on his pipe again, watching both of us in turn. Finally, he tapped the ashes out against his worktable. "Very well. I will say what I know. But I must clarify that I am only mostly sure that the one I speak of is Freya's husband. The one I encountered never identified himself as such."

I glanced at Mercy and we both nodded our understanding.

"I was searching for chromite to use in steel torcs. I travelled throughout that area before moving to the southern lands of Africa." He smiled wryly. "The heat there is preferable to the cold of Siberia."

"I'm sure," I murmured.

"I had just found a trader who had crossed the desert of Syria with his goods. He had a full wagon of chromite, one of the largest, purest stocks I'd ever seen." He pointed with his pipe before popping it back in his mouth. He puffed on the unlit stone for a moment before taking it out and scowling at it.

"I was quite invested in the deal, you see," he explained, pulling out the bag of moss and packing his pipe mechanically. "I only noticed this other man because he was so fair and tall compared to the locals. Light brown hair and beard in the style of the northmen and Aesir, blue eyes. You understand?"

I nodded.

"He was arguing with a Roman who had been standing in the square. The Latin man, a Phoenician by birth, I believe... He preached of the new god. Um, Jesus the Christ, son of the desert god?" The dwarf nodded. "That was it. Yahweh was how the desert god was known back then. Now he is called Jehovah, if he is named at all, as I remember it."

"Yeah, I'm familiar," I said, wryly.

Sviðr nodded. "They argued loudly. Loud enough they were disrupting the trades around them, including mine." He frowned at the memory. "It was very rude and annoying."

"I'm sure it was," I said.

He looked at me, pointing with his pipe. "Never interrupt trade in the desert lands of Midgard," he advised. "They'll cut your throat for that, if they get in a mood. So, we were interrupted, and we stopped to watch." He scratched his nose with one finger. "We had been enjoying the trade and were in a good mood, so we saw it as entertaining." He glared at me. "Still rude, though."

I nodded my agreement, pushing down the hope that rose in my mind.

CHAPTER 32

"So we watched them argue for a time. The Phoenician claimed the Christ was the only god, the true god. Such as some do." He frowned. "It was the fair man's argument that struck me as particularly odd."

"Oh?" I asked, wondering if there would be anything useful in the dwarf's tale. It seemed to be focused on all the wrong things.

"He said that Yahweh and the Christ could leave their followers, and another could step in with a completely different message, and many Christians would still blindly follow, they were so fanatical about their faith." He tapped the stem of the pipe against his lips. "Isn't that an odd thing to say?"

He heaved a sigh. "He went on to claim that the same was true of most gods. They could be replaced by another and most of their followers wouldn't even notice. He said it was the religion that people followed, not the gods, and it was about obedience and not respect."

"Well." I frowned. "That's... very strange. But why do you think it was Odr?"

The dwarf's expression brightened from the thoughtful frown. "Oh, he said something. Let me think. Um. 'My bride wouldn't notice her missing husband, and my king wouldn't miss me any more than I would miss him.' That's what he said, more or less."

Sviðr frowned at the pipe, once again cold in his hand. "And he claimed that the gods didn't honor their brothers, even when kith and kin were supposed to be most important." He muttered as he filled the pipe yet again.

I frowned. "Yeah, that sounds like he's Norse or at least familiar with them." I shook my head. "I don't suppose you have any idea where he went from there?"

"Sure," the dwarf said, absently. He was focused on packing his pipe just right. "He said he wasn't going to rest until he had proven his point throughout the Empire." He furrowed his brow. "I suppose he could have meant something else, but I took it to mean the Roman Empire." He paused, rubbing his bearded chin. "I wonder how far he got."

I shook my head and looked at Mercy. "The Roman Empire? That's long gone. He could be anywhere then."

She nodded. "It doesn't narrow it down much," she said. "But it is more than we had before."

I grimaced. "I suppose. Who hangs out in the middle east?"

Mercy frowned. "From the realms? Mostly fae from Álfheimr or monsters." She sighed. "God creatures, usually from Jötunheimr. Specifically, sandstorm jötun and their adopted kin, the Djinn."

I stood and sighed. "Okay, Jötunheimr it is." I turned to Sviðr, inspiration striking me as I planned my words. "Thank you for the information. This was a good trade."

The dwarf's face split in a full grin. "A good trade, indeed, quest hero." The grin turned bashful. "Or didn't you think I knew?"

I laughed as Mercy and I stepped back into the stream of svartálfar to return to the bifrost. I kept thinking about what Sviðr had said about Odr's argument. Something about it kept drawing me back.

I shook my head. It was probably because of my anxiety over Jehovah hunting me down. All the talk of the god in his early years must have captured my innate curiosity about why he was so focused on me and my quest.

We stepped into the bifrost with that question still hanging in the back of my mind. When the time in the bifrost seemed to drag on for longer than usual, my anxiety got worse. I tried not to panic, knowing the emotional energy spiral that it would cause.

I focused on my breaths, pulling on my memories of Ella and Maria to help me with it. After much longer than I was comfortable with, I felt the tug on my arm, indicating Mercy was pulling us out at our destination.

We stumbled a few steps, then the Valkyrie turned to me.

"Are you okay, Nicola?" Her brow furrowed in a concerned frown.

"Yeah," I said, trying to be casual and dismissive about it. I didn't want it to be a thing. I worried that it was an issue, regardless.

Apparently, Mercy agreed with the latter of my thoughts. "Maybe we should have gone with what you already know instead of searching for more."

I snorted. "What I already know is either not much or locked up." I tapped my head. "I got a peek in the puddle of TMI, sure. But it's just as blocked off as when the ravens-"

I stopped. I had been about to reveal Huginn and Muninn's most important secret. They had been in the astral plane, a place where gods and god creatures shouldn't be able to go. I couldn't tell Mercy that. Which meant I shouldn't mention the memory pearl they had given me...

My eyes widened. They had said I should focus on thought and memory, and the gift they'd given. They had to have been talking about the memory pearl.

I frowned. Skald had known about the memory pearl, but she was a Norn. Nothing was kept from the Norns for long.

I needed to search my mind for the memories from the pearl and the puddle. That's what Huginn and Muninn must have meant. It was the perfect way to describe how I pulled those memories out, too. Thought and memory.

"Damn," I whispered.

"Nicola? What were you saying?"

I looked at Mercy, blinking as I refocused on her face after staring into the distance, lost in thought. "What? What was I saying?"

She shook her head. "Something about being blocked and the ravens did something...?"

"Oh," I said, grasping. "Sandwiches."

"What?"

I sighed. "When you and the ravens brought me sandwiches. I was blocked off. Emotionally and mentally. Right? Same thing here." I frowned. "I think I've thought of something, though."

I looked around, curious about the Jötunheimr realm farther from Loki's cave. Our surroundings were harsh and beautiful in their starkness.

Steep mountains surrounded us, with bare rock cliffs breaking up the pine trees covering the lower portion of the sides. In between lay brownish-green fields with sharp, whipping grasses and spiney brush.

The biting wind blew our hair around our heads. Angry gray clouds covered up the sun, though it still managed to be hot when the chill winds slowed enough.

Out of the corner of my eye, I saw movement. I turned my head to look, but there was nothing there. It happened again, and a third time.

"You won't be able to see them," Mercy said. "Not until they attack."

I swallowed. "This is not where we need to be, is it."

The Valkyrie sighed. "It was where we thought we needed to be, but if you have a better idea."

I caught the movement in the corner of my eye again and nodded. "Let's get out of here."

A creature with more than four legs, no fur, and huge, bat-like ears ran like a housecat toward us. I screamed as Mercy lunged toward me.

CHAPTER 33

The blinding silver-blue light gave me hope that we had made it to the bifrost. The numbness of my limbs prevented me from determining if the swipe I'd seen coming had landed.

I let myself float in the nothingness, trying to come to terms with my own death. Monster from Jötunheimr or poison shutting down my organs while I lay helpless in the hospital. Neither choice was on my list of top ten ways to kick the bucket.

The jerk pulling me out of my passive state wasn't welcome, but it wasn't unwelcome either. I stumbled over my feet and fell to my knees. Looking up, I found Mercy leaning over me, concern written on her face.

"If you do that too long, your face will freeze like that," I muttered.

The Valkyrie frowned. "You must be okay. You are being snarky."

I shrugged, scrambling to my feet. "I'll be snarky until I'm in the grave," I warned. "It isn't a good indicator of my well-being."

She rolled her eyes.

I looked around, recognizing the area. "Hey! We're back at Valhalla. Yay. Full circle."

Mercy nodded. "I figured this was as good a place as any to regroup. Better than most, in fact."

I nodded, suddenly feeling the strain of our grand tour. I hobbled a few feet, exaggerating my exhaustion. "Race ya."

Mercy shook her head. "You would lose."

I nodded. "Yup, but you'd feel better."

She put her arm through mine, and we climbed the hill to the hall of Odin. She pushed me through the doorway without preamble.

"You rest," she said. "Then we continue."

I nodded, making my way through the tables to the room I'd rested in before. It looked the same, and I suddenly felt comfortable.

When I was rested and refreshed, I made my way out to the table where I'd spoken to Mercy and Rade... Had it only been a few days ago?

I shook my head. Time was so fluid and subjective here, I wasn't sure.

Rade was nowhere to be found, and Mercy had already set up a platter of meats, cheeses, fruits and flatbread. As I plopped down beside her, she pushed the food toward me and filled a pair of cups with fruit infused water.

I ate, knowing it was more about feeding my spirit than anything else. The familiar act of eating, though, gave me a sense of calm and rightness in the world. Mercy simply watched and waited.

I took another swig from the cup and smiled at her.

"Better?" she asked.

"Much. It's amazing how one can need a snack even without a body." I grinned.

Her laugh was more relaxed than I'd heard from her in a while.

"So what was that thing?" I asked. "The naked cat creature?"

The Valkyrie shook her head. "I've never seen that one before. I don't know. It seemed... wrong." She frowned. "I've encountered many jötun, many monsters, all around the world. That one was... odd."

I frowned, but Mercy had already changed the subject.

"You said you needed to do something?" she asked. "Or you had an idea?"

I nodded. "I have some knowledge in my mind, but not easily accessed." I caught her curious look. "Skald and the Well of Urdr... You know, that kind of thing. I need to try to access that knowledge, I think. But I'll need quiet time to do so."

"Okay," the Valkryie said. "Just use the room and wherever else you would be comfortable doing that. Let me know when you are done. I'll spread the word that you aren't to be disturbed during that time."

I nodded. "It might take a while," I warned.

Mercy smiled wryly. "Remembering can be like that."

*****

I sat on the bed piled high with furs, wriggling a little to get comfortable. I was reminded of doing this same thing on a hard plastic bench in a jail cell. The chill had kept me from going under for longer, but I'd finally managed it.

I'd gone through a small portion of the memories Huginn and Muninn had given me, hoping for a clue then as now. Over and over, I'd pulled the overwhelming amount of sensory information up, sifting through it for clues. It had taken hours, but I'd gotten enough to guide me when I'd needed it.

Now I needed a similar miracle.

After a while, I felt myself drifting away. I followed the natural path my mind took as it entered the semi-conscious space between everything.

A wave of numbness washed over my limbs and up my neck and jaw. I felt myself falling, free falling, falling into nothing, falling into everything. When I knew I was partially out and able to stay there, I tugged my mind in the direction I wanted.

I recreated the scene. Me, crouched in the roots of Yggdrasil itself, speaking to the Norn. She gestured at the pool of water so close to the well of knowledge where Odin had gleaned the Runes and the spells they created. The physical manifestation of several of those were now on the chain around my neck.

I looked down into the water, unsure of what would happen. I remembered the lights and the voices, and I tugged softly on those memories.

Sights and sounds flooded my mind. I struggled to pick out individual pieces. There were too many, too fast. And the experience ended.

I breathed and refocused the tiny conscious part of my mind back on the task. I recreated the scene. Me, crouched in the roots of Yggdrasil itself, speaking to the Norn.

The memory came easier this time. Easier and more quickly. I plucked at bits of color and sound, but there were too many, too fast. And the experience ended.

I breathed and refocused my mind back on the task. I recreated the scene. Me, crouched in the roots of Yggdrasil itself, speaking to the Norn.

The memory came easier and more quickly. I grasped at bits of color and sound, but there were too many, too fast. And the experience ended.

I breathed and refocused on the task. I recreated the scene, crouched in the roots of Yggdrasil itself. The memory came easier and more quickly.

I grasped an image, though the sound was too muted to hear. Isabel led me to the man in the suit. Her assistant hovered behind her.

There were too many, too fast. And the experience ended.

I breathed and refocused on the task. I recreated the scene, crouched in the roots of Yggdrasil itself. The memory came easier and more quickly.

Isabel introduced me to the man, Mr. Lytle. Her assistant hovered behind her. Leon, his name was.

And the experience ended.

I breathed and refocused on the task. I recreated the scene, crouched among the roots. The memory came easier and more quickly.

I was speaking to Mr. Lytle. We were talking about economics theory and practice. Isabel had disappeared from the scene. I ate spice cake.

And the experience ended.

I breathed and refocused on the task. I recreated the scene. The memory came easier and more quickly.

I spoke to Mr. Lytle. Isabel moved on to another corporate guy. Leon brought us spice cake. Mr. Lytle choked. I passed out muddy water.

And the experience ended.

I breathed and refocused on the task. The memory came easier and more quickly.

Leon brought us spice cake. Mr. Lytle choked. Leon brought in a bag of Fuller's earth. I passed out muddy water.

And the experience ended. I breathed and refocused on the task.

I spoke to Mr. Lytle. Nearby, a pair of protesters spoke about their gardens. One of the women spoke with a heavy Asian accent that I couldn't place.

"You have to be careful with it. Mulching Adelfa will poison the vegetables."

She showed her smartphone to the other woman.

"Oh, yes."

And the experience ended. I breathed and refocused.

"Mulching Adelfa will poison the vegetables." She showed her smartphone to the other woman.

"Oh, yes. That one is very toxic. We call it-"

And the experience ended. I refocused.

"Oh, yes. That one is very toxic. We call it Oleander."

CHAPTER 34

And the experience ended. I refocused, searching again.

Leon brought us the spice cake. Mr. Lytle choked. Leon brought in the bag of Fuller's earth from his gardening truck.

"Mulching Adelfa will poison the vegetables."

And the experience ended. I refocused, searching for more information.

Leon brought in the bag of Fuller's earth from his gardening truck. There was a shiny spot on the bag. I focused hard on it.

Tape. Someone had put tape on the bag.

And the experience ended. I refocused, searching for more.

Leon brought us spice cake. He didn't eat any himself.

Joseph stood nearby, speaking to a woman in a sweater. He shook his head at the offered cake.

I refocused, searching for more.

Leon brought us spice cake. Joseph shook his head. I searched my mind for Isabel, but she was not in the room.

I jerked to full consciousness and fell back against the furs. I lay there for several minutes, thinking about all I'd gotten from my search without really thinking about it.

Finally, I'd processed it enough to keep it all in my mind. I sat up and pursed my lips.

After another few moments, I got off the bed and went in search of a sounding board. Rade and Mercy were not in sight, so I pulled one of the serving men down to sit beside me.

He protested, but I just waggled a cup at him. "Keep it full and let me talk," I told him.

He nodded reluctantly, pouring juice from the sweating pitcher into the cup.

"Adelfa has to be Oleander. That makes sense because Oleander is notoriously poisonous." I smiled. "Well, notorious ever since that movie came out."

"Movie?"

I nodded at the serving man. "So it isn't a huge stretch for a lot of people to know about Oleander. Paraquat is also pretty common, though most don't specifically know the name. They just know that pesticides are poisonous in general."

The serving man blanched and looked around as if searching for help.

I put a hand on his arm. "Just listen," I insisted. "First, we were poisoned with paraquat, which is treated by ingesting Fuller's earth. Dollars to donuts says that the bag of Fuller's earth had been laced with Oleander... um, juice, I guess?" I scratched my head. "The question remains the same, though."

"What's that?" the man asked.

I poked a finger at him. "Who dunnit, of course. I mean, you could ask why, but that's just motive. Cops and lawyers have to worry about that stuff."

I frowned. "Technically, I don't even need to know who dunnit, though. I just need to get the Oleander info to the docs treating us."

I crossed my arms. "How the hell am I supposed to do that?" I demanded. "I'm in a coma. If I try to go back, I'll probably just go fully unconscious with no chance at all of getting the info out."

The man swallowed. I drained my cup and waggled it at him. He filled it hastily.

"Do you even know how hard it is to communicate with someone who isn't there?" I asked him. "I mean, I've only managed it, really and truly, like, once..."

I stared off into space. "That was dangerous, too. I went into Joseph's dream to do it. He nearly strangled me." I glanced at the man.

He'd risen up off the seat as if to leave. When he saw me look at him, he sighed and dropped back down.

"It was an accident," I assured him. "I mean, it's hard to control your dreams when you are trying. He had no idea I would try to contact him that way." I sighed. "But there doesn't seem to be any other way." I frowned at the man, and he started looking around for help again. "I mean, you gotta do what you gotta do, right?" I leaned forward. "Right?"

He nodded violently. "Oh, y-yes. Of c-course, quest hero."

I leaned back, feeling suddenly guilty for dumping on this poor guy. He just wanted to serve his pitcher of juice. "I freaked you out," I said. "Sorry about that. Go on." I waved him off.

He ran around the side of the longhouse, leaving me staring into a half-empty cup. I smirked. Maybe it was half full. "Or maybe it's got juice in it," I muttered, draining it and slamming the cup on the table.

I stood up without looking around and strode away from the longhouse. The only way I knew to navigate into the dream world was through the astral plane, and the only way I knew back to the astral plane was through the bifrost.

I was halfway back to the bifrost when Mercy landed in front of me. I stopped and blinked at her. "Something wrong?" I asked.

"Where are you going, mortal one?" She stood, crossing her arms like she was about to lecture me.

I smiled and stepped around her. "To the bifrost, if it wasn't completely obvious," I said over my shoulder. "What else is this way?" I paused. "Seriously, though. What else is this way?"

Mercy glared at me, falling in step beside me. "The ocean, actually," she said. "And why are you going to the bifrost. You are supposed to be finding out-"

"I know what caused the coma," I said quietly. "I am going to try to communicate that to Joseph in his dreams, so he can, somehow, tell the doctors what to look for." I glanced over at Mercy. "Then, when it's safe to go back to my body, I can finish it, find the poisoner, track down Odr, stop Jehovah, and save the frickin' world."

Mercy stopped in her tracks, while I continued without breaking stride. After a moment, she jogged to catch up again.

"Is that all?" she asked. "I mean, isn't there anything else you want to pile on?"

I frowned. "Well, I do have the rest of the Runespells to find, and I need to figure out how to reconnect with my daughters and resolve my issues with my mother." I glanced at her. "I just figured, one day at a time, right?"

The Valkyrie shook her head. "No wonder you're in therapy."

I nodded soberly. "Facts."

We approached the bifrost and stopped. I turned to face her.

"I guess this is goodbye for now," I said. "I mean, you can't go to the astral plane."

She nodded. "That's right." She frowned. "Be careful, Nicola."

I gave her a half smile. "Don't worry. You're not going to lose your quest hero this easily."

Mercy shook her head. "I don't worry about you as the quest hero, Nicola. I worry about you as a friend." She reached out to hug me.

I hugged her right back, feeling the burn begin in my eyes. "Now, don't be making me cry," I said. "I'll melt, you know."

She rolled her eyes. "You aren't that sweet."

I laughed. "Nope, but I am salty ay-eff."

She nodded, laughing with me. "Stay safe. Don't let that bestie of yours try to kill you in his sleep again."

I saluted. Unwilling to continue drawing out the farewell, I simply stepped into the bifrost once more.

CHAPTER 35

I stepped out into the astral plane and gave myself only a moment to reorient. Then I stepped out of the astral, shifting worlds around me.

A lurch warned me of what was coming before the scene cleared before my eyes. Satan was striding toward me across the soft, green grass. He had an unpleasant smile on his face and his eyes glinted with anger.

I shook my head. "Sorry, Luci. No time to play, now. I have grown-up things to do."

A thought struck me just before I stepped through the worlds again. I looked at the god thoughtfully as he came closer. "On second thought, I do have a question for you."

The gorgeous face flickered with confusion for a brief moment. Then he continued toward me without a word.

I smiled. "Does it bother you that I'm getting very close to finding him?"

Satan frowned. "Who's that, mortal?"

I grinned. "Why, Odr, of course."

I stepped sideways before he could get closer. Just before the scene swept away, I saw his face change to complete shock tinged with fear.

"Gotcha," I muttered. "I knew there was a connection."

The worlds stopped shifting and I was floating in the dream world once more. It was familiar, though it felt like it had been years since I'd been here. I let myself float for a moment, sending out delicate touches of energy to examine the dreams nearest to me. None of them were familiar people.

Then one of the dreams turned dark. I paused, looking closer at it. The dreamer's energy wasn't familiar, but the scene in the dream was. It was the meeting between the energy corporation and the protesters. I watched in fascinated horror as the dreamer ate a piece of spice cake, then began to choke.

They dreamt of people leaning over them as they struggled, laughing. In the background, Isabel and Leon were fighting to get to the dreamer, to save them.

I pulled back from the dream. The topic was drawing me in too far, and there was no way to know if the dream was accurate to what had really happened.

I blinked, finding myself surrounded by dozens of other dreams. They crowded around me, trying to draw me in. I peeked into each one, and they were all about the meeting, about the poisoning. I frowned. I was getting too close to them. I recentered myself and drew back emotionally and energetically. Space opened up around me, slowly.

Finally, I felt that the dreams were far enough away to risk travelling through the dream world. I closed my eyes and pictured Joseph. I pulled in everything I knew about him, every emotion I had for him.

I felt the wash of sorrow when he had been shot along the Appalachian Trail. I felt the stab of betrayal when we'd fought on the same trip. And I felt the comfort of his presence when I told him everything and he simply accepted it.

I opened my eyes and looked around. Only one dream was nearby, and I could feel the familiarity of the dreamer already.

I smiled. Joseph.

I took a deep breath, hoping this time I wouldn't be strangled by vines. I dove into his dream.

*****

I was in a bed. Machines beeped around me. A mask covered my mouth. Wires and tubes restrained my arms and legs. I blinked rapidly, trying to focus.

Doctors filled the room, busy but doing nothing. Joseph stood in the midst of it all, staring at me. Tears ran down his face.

"Nicola, don't die," he sobbed.

I struggled against the equipment that effectively tied me down. I pulled at wires and tubes, wincing when my tugging yanked a huge needle from my arm. I pulled the mask off my face at last.

"Joseph!"

He looked at me, and his expression crumbled.

Machines beeped around me. A mask covered my mouth. Wires and tubes restrained my arms and legs.

Doctors filled the room, busy but doing nothing. Joseph stood in the midst of it all, tears running down his face.

"Nicola, don't die," he sobbed.

I flexed, pulling at my magic and using the energy to pull away from the wires and tubes. I pulled the mask off my face at last.

"Joseph!"

He looked at me, and his expression crumbled.

Machines beeped around me. A mask covered my mouth. Wires and tubes wrapped around my arms and legs. Doctors filled the room, busy but doing nothing. Joseph stood, tears running down his face.

"Nicola, don't die," he sobbed.

I reached for him with tendrils of energy, willing him to get my message.

"Joseph!"

His eyes met mine and I narrowed my eyes, willing time to slow before the scene reset again.

Time enough for another single word. "Oleander."

He looked at me and his expression crumbled.

Machines beeped around me. A mask covered my mouth. Wires and tubes wrapped around my limbs. Doctors filled the room. Joseph stood, tears running down his face.

"Nicola, don't die," he sobbed.

I reached for him with tendrils of energy, willing him to get my message. "Joseph!"

His eyes met mine and I narrowed my eyes, willing time to slow before the scene reset again.

"Oleander."

He looked at me and his expression crumbled.

Machines beeped. A mask covered my mouth. Wires and tubes wrapped around my arms and legs. Doctors filled the room. Joseph stood, tears running down his face.

"Nicola, don't die," he sobbed.

I reached for him with tendrils of energy, willing him to get my message.

"Joseph!"

His eyes met mine.

"Oleander."

Machines beeped, and I was lost in the endless loop of the dream.

*****

Blackness swallowed me at last, and I floated, adrift in nothing.

The nothing tickled my cheek.

I opened my eyes to frown at the nothing. I blinked in the unexpected light. I tried to lift my hand to brush away the nothing that tickled my cheek, but my limbs wouldn't move.

I frowned into the room, into the unexpected light. I frowned at it until it faded away into blackness once more.

CHAPTER 36

I lifted my head, wondering that it felt so heavy. I must have fallen into Joseph's dream and drained most of my energy off for my spirit to be so heavy. I tried to open my eyes, but they didn't respond.

I sighed and let myself drift away once more.

*****

My eyes fluttered open, and I frowned at the scene before them. Where in the spirit world was I that I was in bed looking out a window?

It wasn't my bed. It wasn't my window. It wasn't the room I'd used in Valhalla. I blinked and stared at the view. Were those skyscrapers?

A door slammed, and I flinched at the loud sound. Then I noticed the other sounds.

Machines beeped around me. I rolled my eyes to look around. There were wires and tubes flowing toward me from the machines.

I moved my mouth. It felt dry. There was a silicon oxygen mask on it. I could feel the steady flow of cold air on my chapped lips.

Dammit. How was I still in Joseph's dream?

I rolled my head to the side and frowned at how heavy it was. I could barely move it. The room was empty. No doctors bustling around doing nothing. No Joseph crying over me.

I rolled my eyes to look farther to the side. I could see the door, half-closed. The opening was blocked by the privacy curtain around the bed.

I groaned and shifted my weight. Correction. I let out a dry croak that was trying to be a groan, and I tried to shift my weight, but none of my muscles responded.

I took a deep breath, not even having the energy to sigh. My eyes followed the tangle of tubes, wires and string from various sources, over the safety arm of the bed, and toward my useless body.

I frowned. String?

I concentrated on the string. It was important somehow.

I dozed off.

My eyes fluttered open, and I rolled my eyes around the room.

Still empty.

String. String was important.

Why was string important? Wires were important. They sent information from sensors to machines to make sure everything was hunky dory.

Tubes were important. They provided fluids and nutrition. Keeping the organs going.

Organs. Organs were important. Organs in danger. Poison.

I gasped as the panic flowed over me for several minutes. One beep beeped faster. I listened to the beep. It calmed me down.

String. String was important. Why? What did string do?

I thought back to every time I'd been in the hospital. I grimaced. It was a lot of times, especially over the last few years.

String wasn't always in the hospital. String pulled on the lights. String was sometimes replaced by a button. A button for drinks and snacks and questions. A call button.

I fumbled my fingers through a tangle of wires and tubes, looking for the fabric-y feel of string. When I found it, I just held it for a moment. I was tired already from looking for the string, thinking about the string.

I was afraid I'd doze off again before I could pull the string. I took another deep breath, feeling slightly dizzy from the oxygen.

I pulled the string. I heard a click. I felt myself drifting off, exhausted from pulling the string. Some quest hero I was. My eyes drifted shut. I heard a squeak of something on the linoleum. I wrenched my eyes open.

A woman stared down at me. She wore pink scrubs. Her eyes widened when she saw my eyes open. Then she grinned.

"Well, well," she said, cheerfully. "Look who's awake. Welcome back to the land of the living."

I tried to smile, but I fell asleep instead.

*****

I sat up with help from the nurse. She'd said her name, but I couldn't remember it. Several people had come in and told me their names. I didn't remember any of them.

The mask had been removed, though it still sat nearby, just in case. I'd drunk a full liter of water trying to wet my mouth. Now, I was going to get food. My expectations were low. I mean, I'd have loved a steak, but I knew I'd get down only a bite or two before my body revolted. It wasn't ready for that kind of work yet.

The nurse lifted the cover off the plate, and I raised my brows.

"Broth and jello," she said. "Diet of champions."

"Champions of what?" I asked, unable to keep the dismay out of my voice.

She grinned. "Champions of not dying from two poisons at once."

I nodded. "I'll take it," I croaked.

I coughed and accepted the water she offered. Then I ate all my jello and the broth like a good patient. At least it was red jello.

She gave me the TV remote before she left, and I flipped through the stations until I found something I could tolerate. I stared at the TV until I fell asleep again.

"Nicola?"

I opened my eyes to find Joseph peering into my face.

His expression immediately brightened, and he hugged me tightly. "I thought-" He stopped and pulled away, sniffling. "I mean, you scared the crap out of me."

I smiled weakly. "Yeah, well. It's kinda my thing these days."

He frowned. "It was really touch and go for a while. With all of you. I didn't know what to do. I was thinking about it constantly."

"He was bugging us constantly," the nurse said, coming back to check my vitals. "He asked about this and that." She scowled at him. "The internet isn't a medical opinion."

Joseph smiled. "You didn't say that the last time."

The nurse nodded. "That was inspired, I must admit."

I watched them, lost but fascinated. "Last time?"

The nurse smiled at me, shining a light into my eyes to check my pupils. "He came in asking if we'd considered there being two poisons. He almost got himself arrested when he suggested oleandrin." She shot him a look.

"Why would he get arrested for suggesting that?" I asked. Something about the conversation was tickling the back of my mind.

The nurse leaned over the bed to feel my neck. "Because that's what it was. The lab found it laced through the bag of Fuller's earth that was used to treat the paraquat."

I stared at Joseph, jumbled memories filling my head.

"The cops decided it was accidental," Joseph said, patting my hand reassuringly. "Runoff from a compost heap that had oleander in it had tainted the ground where the Fuller's earth had been collected." He grimaced. "At least, that's the theory."

The nurse shook her head, making some notes on my chart. She smiled at both of us before leaving with a warning to not wear me out.

"You dreamt it," I accused Joseph as soon as she was gone.

His eyes widened. "So it was you sneaking into my dreams again." He narrowed his eyes at me playfully. "I'm gonna start dreaming in porn, just to keep you out."

I snorted. "Joke's on you if you think that would keep me out." I waggled a finger at him. "I had a mission, you know."

He smiled. "Well, mission accomplished."

I frowned. "I'm not so sure about that." I wasn't sure what I meant by that, but I was certain I didn't want to think about it right now.

CHAPTER 37

My mother brought the girls in the next day. I was still trying to figure out what else there was about the situation that I was supposed to deal with. It felt important, but the constant fatigue of recovering weighed down my thoughts.

I hugged Ella and Maria tightly when they threw themselves at me. Tears burned in my eyes.

"You know what?" I asked them. "You both were what I kept thinking about this whole time."

Ella frowned. "You were unconscious, Mama."

I nodded. "I was in a coma, but I taught myself a long time ago to be conscious when I'm unconscious."

"Like in a dream?" Maria asked.

"Exactly," I said, touching the tip of her nose with my finger. "I knew I was unconscious, just running around inside my mind. But I knew you were waiting for me, and so I kept fighting to come back."

Maria grinned and Ella blushed.

"Do you know why?" I asked.

Ella leaned in and whispered so that only Maria and I could hear her. "Is it 'cause you love us, Mama?"

I couldn't keep the tears from spilling at her words. My throat closed up and I could only nod emphatically while I pulled them closer. "That's exactly it," I croaked into their hair.

Maria pulled back and grinned. "We love you, too, Mama. We really are glad you didn't die." She glanced at Ella, then back at my mother.

The older woman sat stiffly in the visitor's chair, watching us without expression. Ella elbowed Maria gently and frowned at her, also glancing at my mother. I narrowed my eyes for a moment, then asked them what they'd been doing while I was sleeping.

They told me about shows and trips to the museum down the street, going to a movie, and shopping for get-well presents for me. That meant it was time for me to get my presents, and I ooh'ed and aah'ed over the giant stuffed teddy and cards filled with hand-written notes.

Afterward, the girls ran off to check out the vending machine, leaving me alone with my mother. I couldn't help thinking of how she had used the Runespell against me for so long. The betrayal of that was still fresh in my mind.

"So, another vacation turned into another life-or-death struggle," she said at last. "I shouldn't be surprised."

"What does that mean? Are you suggesting I deserved this? Or was asking for it?" I narrowed my eyes at her.

She shrugged. "I don't pretend to know what you want, Nicola. I've never understood you or your reasons." She adjusted her jacket on her shoulders. "But you do have a tendency of ending up in these kinds of situations. I can't help but wonder why."

"So you do think I'm asking for it," I said quietly. I could feel my rage simmering just under the surface. "Like I wanted to be poisoned. Like I wanted to be left helpless, to leave my girls without me."

My mother lifted a shoulder. "Well, it would explain things."

I scowled. "I don't know why I'm surprised."

"What is that supposed to mean?"

I pressed my lips together for a moment, trying to pull myself back from the anger. "You are so busy trying to blame me for what has happened to me, you never actually try to help me get through it all."

She rolled her eyes, infuriating me even more. "You need to take responsibility-"

I cut her off, not willing to listen to her blame-game again. "I get shot at, and it's my fault. I get poisoned, and it's my fault. Gods, Mom, everything is my fault, isn't it?" I glared at her. "Maybe Dad dying is my fault, too?"

She glared right back at me. "Are you admitting something?"

I threw up my hands. "You know, after all the crap that has happened to me, the one reaction I would have expected from my own mother is that you would at least be happy I lived." I hesitated a moment. "But are you?"

"What is that supposed to mean?" She stood abruptly and started pacing.

I kept my eyes on her, watching her. "Are you at all happy I'm not dead? Or do you wish I'd died in any of these situations?"

She rolled her shoulders in a half shrugging motion. "Of course I don't want you to die-"

"But are you happy I didn't die?" I pushed.

"Look," she said, turning to face me. "I have a reputation, you know. People know me. People know about me. And you. People ask me about you. What am I supposed to say?"

I just stared at her.

"I barely know how to explain that you were in a shootout. Then there was that man who attacked us in your house. You put him in a coma, Nicola. You beat him until he was no longer alive in so many ways. You caught an escaped prisoner on vacation. You-" She choked on the words. "That poor woman on the island. What you did to her..." She shook her head and began pacing again. "How do I explain that to people? People I have to live with in our town."

"I live there, too, you know," I said quietly. "I have to deal with it, too. Thanks to you, I have to live through all of that stuff, then live knowing even my own mother doesn't want me to have lived."

"Now, Nicola-"

"Maybe you should leave," I said. "Just... pack up and go home." I sat up. "I'll hire someone to watch the girls with Joseph. When I get home, I'll contact a real estate agent and get the house listed."

"You're moving?" My mom went pale. "What about the girls?"

I pressed my lips together. "I think some time away from you will do us all some good."

She frowned. "By us, you don't include me."

I glared at her. "You removed yourself from my family a while ago," I said. "I'm just not going to fight that anymore."

She pressed her lips together. "You can't take away my granddaughters. They are all I have left."

I stared at her. "No, Mom. You had me, too."

I continued to stare at her as she began crying. Finally, she left, sobbing softly.

I let my head fall, pushing the emotions away. She didn't deserve my sorrow. But it wasn't her that I wanted to cry over. It was the loss of the idea of my relationship with my mother. That's what I wanted to mourn.

Finally, I let those tears fall. Once it started, it didn't stop. I was sobbing uncontrollably by the time Joseph came in.

CHAPTER 38

"We just need to ask you some questions, Ms. Crandall."

I blinked up at the detective who stood poised over my bed. She had a small notebook cradled in one hand while the other held a pen ready to scratch down notes.

"Shoot," I said. "I don't remember a lot. I'm still a bit foggy on the whole thing."

The sharply dressed woman smiled. "That's fine. We'll just see what comes up."

I mentally applauded her optimism while wondering if there was actually more information hiding in the depths than I knew. I nearly rolled my eyes at myself for that thought.

Of course there was. Half my adventures were stashed in psychological boxes rather than letting my mind be overwhelmed by the emotions, or even the sheer amount of information. I briefly flashed to a memory of a puddle surrounded by roots and branches.

Instead, I relaxed against the pillows and waited for the questioning to begin.

"Why were you at the meeting in the first place?"

I sucked on one of my eyeteeth for a moment before answering. "I was in town for a conference. Herbalism. And we had gotten here a few days early."

"We?"

"Me and Joseph and my daughters," I clarified. "We came to check out some of the sights. I got lost trying to find a vineyard. We came upon a protest and stopped to ask directions. Then we ended up chatting with the lady in charge and she invited us to come to the meeting."

"Why you?"

I shrugged. "I think she was looking for more people. She seemed impressed by how well we could talk about it without having been involved. Maybe she just wanted some new faces, or more perspectives."

"And you decided to go?"

I shrugged again. "It sounded entertaining. And there was food." I grinned. "I spent too much time as a poor college student to turn down a free meal."

The detective scratched down her notes as I spoke, the sound of the pen grating on my nerves. "And then what happened? What did you do at the meeting?"

I thought for a moment, trying to remember. "We started with the buffet table, then Isabel and Leon found us. They introduced me to a man who was wanting to talk about economic impact." I smiled. "I kinda jumped into the convo with both feet."

"Did your conversation get hostile at any point?"

"Nope."

The detective scratched more notes. "And the man's name?"

"Umm, he was a CFO," I murmured. "Little? Lytle? Something like that."

The detective nodded. "What about other conversations around you? Did you notice anyone getting angry or bursting out yelling?"

I considered for a moment. "No, nothing like that. Everyone seemed to be on their best behavior. Polite, maybe passionate, but nothing aggressive."

"And what about the cake?"

"Cake?" I frowned. "You mean, the spice cake?" I shrugged. "Leon brought me a piece. I ate it. The rest is... well, you know."

"Leon brought you the cake? You didn't get it from the buffet table?"

I nodded. "I just figured he was passing it all out to be nice."

"Did he eat a piece?"

"Not that I saw, I don't think."

"And Isabel. Did she eat any cake?"

"I don't know," I said. "Wouldn't they have been in the hospital like the rest of us if they had?"

The detective nodded absently. "Probably, but we can't find either of them. We don't know for sure."

My eyebrows raised at that. "Can't find them? So they just... vanished?"

She nodded again. "The cake was made at a local bakery. Our investigation shows that the paraquat was likely added in liquid form after the cake was purchased. It was brought to the meeting by an older woman, a Mrs. Treyman. She was one of the unfortunate fatalities, so we are assuming she didn't poison the cake, or she likely wouldn't have eaten it."

I nodded.

"So you ate the cake. Then what?"

I frowned. "Mr. Little started choking. Other people did the same. Then I saw Leon carrying a bag. It was Fuller's Earth. We started making a sludge with the Fuller's Earth and water and juice pitchers from the buffet."

"You were helping with this?"

I nodded. "Several people were."

The detective scratched more notes. "So it wasn't just one person in charge of the treatment."

"No. We were all grabbing things as fast as we could."

"Including Leon?"

I nodded. "He was showing us how much to add to the liquid."

The detective nodded.

"Does that mean something?" I asked.

She shook her head. "Maybe. If there were many people working on the treatment, it's not likely that the mixing of the sludge, as you called it, was the point of the second poisoning. It must have been before that."

I nodded. "It was chaotic. People were panicking and trying to help all over the place."

"Did you see Isabel during that time?"

I frowned. "I don't think so. I wasn't really paying attention."

The woman nodded. "Okay, I think that's about it for my questions." She looked me in the eye. "Is there anything else you remember that might help us catch this person?"

I shook my head slowly. "I don't think..." An image flashed through my mind. "Oh! Tape!"

"Tape?"

I sat up straighter. "Tape. There was a piece of clear tape on the bag that Leon carried in. Like it had a hole in it or something. I don't know why I noticed it. I was probably just hyper focusing on little things to avoid the chaos around me."

The detective nodded. "We do have the remainder of the bag of Fuller's Earth in evidence. I'll make a note to check it for punctures sealed with tape. That would likely be how they introduced the second poison."

She pulled out a business card and handed it over to me. "If you think of anything else, call me."

I nodded. "I hope you find whoever did this."

The detective nodded but she didn't seem very hopeful. I tried not to feel dejected by that. I couldn't help but think that until we understood who did the poisoning and why, I wouldn't feel completely safe about moving on.

CHAPTER 39

I was released from the hospital a few days later. The most daunting thing about it was the diagnosis I received as a result of my double-poisoning.

On top of it nearly killing many of us, it left me with a weakened heart. I was to watch for signs, such as shortness of breath, fatigue and loss of focus. I heaved a sigh as I tucked the information into my bag to go through later. As if getting older wasn't bad enough.

The girls were excited to have me back with them. Joseph had kept them busy with sightseeing, but everyone was tired of living out of the hotel. We booked a flight home and settled in to wait the few days until we would leave.

It only took a few hours before the drama found us again.

I answered as the pounding on the door started up a second time. The sight of Leon in the hallway shocked me.

"What the hell are you doing here?" I demanded. "How did you even find me?"

Leon pushed past me and closed the door. "I'm so sorry. I had to find someone who might know what really happened."

"What are you talking about?"

Joseph peeked his head around the doorframe into the girls' bedroom where the three of them had been continuing the movie we'd sat down to watch. "Any trouble?"

"Dunno," I grumbled. "Leon here was just about to explain why he shows up at our hotel and makes himself at home in our room."

Joseph stepped out into the common room. "Oh really?"

I smothered a grin. Joseph was tall and pretty well-built in appearance, but he was a giant teddy bear. He was trying to be intimidating, knowing the whole time that I was more of a threat to anyone wanting trouble.

Leon fell for it though. He swallowed and backed up a step before turning to me. "Please. I need your help."

"With what?" I asked.

The man glanced at Joseph. "The cops are trying to pin this whole thing on me."

Joseph crossed his arms, and I followed suit. "Are you saying you didn't do it?" Joseph demanded.

Leon shook his head. "Look. I keep Fuller's Earth on my truck for my business. I'm always using it for my landscaping business. It's a good filler. Adding poison, especially oleander, would kill off or contaminate most of the plants wherever it's used. It would be useless to me."

"Unless you knew it would be used to treat the other poison," I pointed out.

Leon frowned. "Why would I poison anyone? I was happy with how much we were getting through to the company's reps. We were going to make a difference. A big difference, in my opinion. Any harm to them or us would just be a set-back."

I frowned at that. "So you thought things were going well?"

Leon shrugged. "I've been doing this for almost two decades," he explained. "We don't get big overhaul changes. Ever. I've learned to take the baby steps for the wins they are, and just hope that enough of them happen to make those bigger changes over time."

"Still, it must be frustrating," Joseph pointed out.

"Frustrating?" Leon laughed. "Yeah, it is. But we go out for drinks and bitch about it. If we take out most of the suits in a company, they'll just hire more suits, and we'll be back at square one. It is frustrating, but that's the game."

I raised my eyebrows. "So you just happened to be the one passing out the cake? You just happened to be the one with a bag of Fuller's Earth? Which just happened to be laced with oleander?"

Leon shook his head. "Isabel suggested we pass out a nice munchie to get everyone in a more productive mindset. You know, sweeten the pot. People listen better when they are in a good mood."

"But why that cake?" Joseph asked.

The man shrugged. "We just... picked it."

I frowned. "Did you pick it or did Isabel?"

"I don't remember. We did exchange words on how much we both like spice cake."

"But neither of you had any?" I asked.

Leon frowned. "I had a bite before things started going downhill. It was a corner piece, so it must have been a section without any of the pesticide in it."

"Convenient," Joseph muttered, standing tall over the shorter man.

Leon flinched at his words. "Yeah, I know." He moved to the sofa and sat down. "I don't know how to explain it. I didn't do this. Don't you remember anything else about that day?"

I frowned, thinking of the tape on the bag. "Well, there was a conversation about oleander nearby. I don't remember who was talking, but it was two women. They were discussing compost and how you shouldn't put oleander in your compost piles."

Leon nodded. "That's pretty common for gardeners and farmers to know around here. It would suck to have your entire crop made toxic because you had one of those get mixed up in your soil. Oleander is pretty, so some people encourage its growth not knowing how much of a pain it is later."

He looked at me expectantly for a moment, but I just shrugged. I couldn't remember much else from that night. At least not that would help him.

"If it wasn't you, then who would it be?" Joseph asked.

"I don't know," Leon murmured. "Isabel is the other obvious choice, but she wouldn't do it for the same reasons I wouldn't do it. I feel like someone is setting us up. Getting busted for something like this would affect public perception of what we are trying to accomplish. It could be as simple as sabotage in the name of negative press."

"It didn't help that you and Isabel just up and vanished, either," I pointed out. "Do you know where she is?"

Leon shook his head. "No. We'd both been questioned about the initial poisoning, then I went home. I haven't seen her since. When it came out that the Fuller's Earth had been poisoned, too, I knew how that would look. I didn't know what to do, so I took off." He rolled his shoulders. "I guess I thought I could find something to clear my name before the cops caught up to me."

I shook my head. "Maybe you should just turn yourself in. Let them know you will help in any way you can. I'm sure they won't press charges until they get some solid evidence."

Leon sighed. "With the way it's been going, that solid evidence will point to me and Isabel the same as everything else that's come out so far."

I sat next to him and reached out to pat his hand. His phone rang, startling both of us. Leon shot me a grimace as he dug the phone out of his pants pocket. He frowned at the screen before answering the call.

"Hello? Isabel? Where are you? ... Have you seen- ... I don't know. ... No, I haven't said- ... What? Where? ... Are you sure? ... Hold tight. I'll get there as soon as I can."

I stared at Leon as he put his phone back into his pocket. "Well?"

He glanced from me to Joseph and back to me. "Isabel. She wants to talk about what happened. She seems to think I might have sold her out or something. I have to meet with her so we can tackle this together."

I glanced at Joseph. He strode towards the door to grab his jacket. "I'll take him. Nicola, you stay with the girls and try not to get into trouble while I'm gone."

I shot him an innocent look. "Trouble? Me? Never." I walked him and Leon to the door. "Stay safe and keep me posted."

Joseph nodded before they both disappeared down the hallway.

CHAPTER 40

Joseph texted when they arrived at the meeting with Isabel. He included the address and a picture. It was a cafe filled with people.

I was nervous for him, but there was nothing really urgent about the feeling. I sat on the bed to watch the movie with the girls, holding my phone in my hands. It bothered me that I had to let Joseph go out into a possibly dangerous situation. But, at the same time, I was still technically in recovery.

A knock sounded at the door, startling me. I told the girls to stay in the bedroom and went to answer it. Joseph might be back and forgot his hotel key. Or it could be the towels we'd called for.

I opened the door, still half-thinking about the possible whos. It took me a moment to process my confusion at seeing Isabel standing there. She pulled her hand out of her jacket pocket and pointed the small revolver at me.

My mind raced. The girls were in the back room, but that was a tentative safety for them. Even if someone heard a shot, they might not want to get involved, or might think it was a movie.

There was the front desk and cameras, but that wouldn't help me now, and there was the weight room door that went out the back. It always seemed to be propped open so the smoking crowd could get back in easily.

Isabel closed the door behind us and waved me over to the sofa. "Sit down," she growled.

I raised my eyebrows as I perched on the edge of the sofa cushion. "Not just gonna shoot and run? Interesting."

The woman glared at me. "You and your tall friend have been a pain in my ass since we met." She cocked the hammer. "I just want to know what you told the cops and doctors. They shouldn't have been able to figure out the poisons fast enough to save anyone. But your friend knew. How?"

I shrugged. "I told him."

Lights flashed behind my eyes before I could register the pain of the slap on my face. "Liar!"

I put my hand against the throb in my cheek. "Ow. What was that for?"

Isabel leaned forward to sneer in my face. "You are lying!"

"Mama?"

I looked behind the woman and my heart dropped into my gut. "Go back to the movie, girls. I'll just be a minute."

Isabel glanced at Ella and Maria. They were standing in the door but closed it when I waved my hand at them. I noticed the woman had blocked their view of the gun with her body.

Great. More therapy for my daughters.

"You are lying," she hissed.

I glared at Isabel, wondering how to get out of this without the girls getting hurt. My thighs began to ache from the tension I was holding in them, so I began cycling through relaxing and flexing the muscles in my legs. "I'm not."

"You couldn't have told your friend. First off, you had no way of knowing for yourself. Second, you were in a coma. You couldn't communicate with anyone."

I shrugged. "I found out. And then I told him."

Isabel rolled her eyes. "How exactly did you discover the nature of the poisons used when you were in a coma?"

I forced my upper body to visibly relax. If I was going to waste time, at least I could try to get her off-balance in the process. "Well, we already knew what the first poison was. Remember? We treated it with the Fuller's Earth."

Isabel smirked. "Naturally. I was aware that so many people with gardening backgrounds would recognize pesticide poisoning. I also knew that someone would know how to treat it."

I smirked back at her. "So you anticipated that by poisoning the cure."

She waved the gun in my face. "But you shouldn't have known that. How did you find out? Who told you?"

I shrugged. "Loki."

The woman blinked. "What? Who?"

I smiled up at her, going for an innocent expression. "Loki. God of mischief."

She scowled. "From the movies?"

I waved a hand dismissively. "Nah. That's comic book Loki. Whole different person. I mean the real god, Loki."

Isabel frowned. "Loki isn't real."

I raised my eyebrows as far as they would go. "Not real? But you're Pagan. Wait, are you one of those non-theists?"

The woman snorted. "Belief in gods is for children."

I shrugged. "I don't judge other people's experiential knowledge of the spirit world," I murmured.

"Stop trying to change the subject," Isabel yelled. "Just tell me how you knew about the oleander!"

I peered up at her without expression. She was so desperate and angry, I wasn't sure what she would do. I just knew that I suddenly felt very sorry for her. "I told you," I said evenly.

"Loki?" she railed. "You expect me to believe that some random god just happened to know about my plans and then found you and told you?"

"No," I said. "I went to him. In Jötunheim. He's bound until Ragnarök, after all. He can't exactly travel the Nine Worlds."

Isabel rolled her eyes. She was getting more frustrated, which made her more erratic. That was good because she would be more likely to make a mistake. It was bad because that mistake could be shooting me... or the girls. I knew I was walking a thin line, but it was all I could think of doing.

She leaned toward me, waving the gun in front of my face. "Do you really expect me to believe that?"

"No, not really," I said. "And, to be completely truthful, Loki didn't tell me. He pointed out some things. Then I did a memory dive and figured it out for myself."

Her eyes narrowed. "Are you messing with me?"

"No," I said.

"Then how the hell did you know?"

I heaved a breath. "Once more, with feeling. Loki pointed out some stuff. I used that as a focal point while I went through my memories of the meet-up. Several things just... came together to point to oleander."

Isabel frowned.

"Oh, but Loki did say it was Adelfa, which is another name for Oleander," I added. "So I guess Loki did tell me."

"You are messing with me," the woman growled. "You have to be."

"There were a few women talking about Oleander in compost heaps at the meet-up. There was tape over the hole in the bag of Fuller's Earth." I stopped and stared at her for a long moment. "Hope that tape doesn't have your fingerprint on it."

The backhand was so sudden, I didn't even see her move before my head whipped to the side.

"You are lying to me!"

CHAPTER 41

My vision shifted to yellow, and I took several deep breaths to try to pull the berserker under control. "I wouldn't do that again," I muttered.

"How did you get the information to your friend?" Isabel demanded.

I shrugged. "I spoke to him in his dreams."

"Liar! That's not possible." The woman's face was turning shades of red and purple as she grew more enraged. She brandished the gun in my face. "I will shoot you. Keep lying and you will regret it."

I narrowed my eyes at her. "Keep threatening me and you will regret it."

She cocked the gun again and pushed the end of it into my cheek. I pushed down the shot of terror that went through me and kept staring into her eyes.

"Tell me how you did it," she said again.

"Why? You won't believe me this time." I bit out the flippant words.

"If you don't tell me the truth, I will shoot you," she said. Staring into my face, she seemed to realize her words weren't going to affect me. "I will shoot those girls, then."

Her immediate smirk told me that I hadn't kept the emotion off my face at her words. She had landed the blow, but I just stared at her. The smirk slid from her expression and the gun tip wobbled against my cheek.

"I told you," I growled, slowly standing up. "You have your answers. You did the wrong thing, and you screwed up worse by trying to threaten me." I rolled my shoulders as the power of the cat flowed through my muscles. "Now you have one chance to get out of here with your skin intact." I pulled at the chain around my neck, lifting the Runespells on it out of the neck of my shirt. "Where's the pendant?"

"How did you kno-" Isabel gulped. "Your eyes..."

She visibly struggled to pull herself together. I simply advanced slowly.

"I-I just wanted to save everyone," she whimpered. "That company will never stop polluting our world. Killing us, slowly."

I reached up and, with one finger, pushed the gun barrel to the side. "So that gives you the right to kill some of us quickly? Fuck you and your righteous cause."

The woman seemed to draw in on herself for a moment, then she recovered and pulled the gun back to point at my head again. She lifted her chin. "I am okay with some collateral damage. This," she pulled a thin chain around her own neck, showing me the familiar shape of a Runespell, "was the sign it was time to act."

"You knew you could ingest the poison without it affecting you, and you took that as a sign you should poison everyone?" I snorted. "And people think I'm crazy?"

She straightened and opened her mouth again. I was certain she was going to try to make her case again, though she might have intended to get back to interrogating me. It didn't matter. I was done.

My eyes closed as I focused for a split second. I pulled on the power of the cougar to get the speed I would need. My eyes snapped open, my vision tinted yellow with a red aura at the edges.

"What are you?" she whispered, staring.

One arm swept in an arc in front of me to knock the gun aside. The other shot out, the heel of my palm connecting with her nose.

The gun dropped to the floor and Isabel bent double, clutching her nose. I grabbed her, kicking the gun away as I moved forward. With a quick twist, I had her arm bent up behind her back.

"Now," I snarled. "That's more like it."

"W-what are you going to do to me?" she whined.

I rolled my eyes. "Sweet baby Baldr, you are too much." I used the leverage I had on her arm to move her closer to the couch. I snatched up my phone and struggled to get it open one-handed. "I'm calling the cops."

She sagged in my grasp. "What are you?" she asked again.

I hesitated, considering the question. "I don't know anymore." I reached around and grabbed the silver pendant from her neck. Time slowed and Odin's voice chanted in my mind.

"I have learned the sixth spell: if poison is used against me, from stone or plant or living creature, that deadly substance will turn to bitter salt in my mouth, and death will not come for me."

Time moved forward, and I slapped the Runespell against my chest, letting the magical chain do the work of holding it. The hotel room door burst open. I jerked Isabel in front of me before my mind processed the two standing in the door.

Leon gaped at the scene from behind Joseph. My bestie, however, took in everything, heaved a sigh, and looked at me. "Can I call the cops now, or do you need a moment?"

I shrugged, a smile tugging at the corner of my mouth. "Now is good." When Joseph rolled his eyes, I snorted. "You're just butt-hurt that I didn't need saving this time."

"This time?" Joseph snorted right back, poking at his phone screen as he spoke. "When is the last time you actually did need saving?"

I shrugged. "Sorry. That's what you get for being friends with a quest hero."

"Oh, please, no. Don't stroke my ego. Not that. Anything but that." His deadpan voice brought another grin to my face.

"Can you check the girls quick?" I asked.

His expression immediately changed to worry. "Oh, shit."

The police arrived in record time and took both Isabel and Leon in, though the poor man would likely be released within the hour with the statements from me and Joseph. Joseph assured the officers that a full deposition would be coming the next day.

When he finally closed the door behind them, I dropped onto the couch. My legs could no longer hold me up.

"Ella! Maria!" I called. When they came up to me, I grabbed them both and pulled them into a hug. "I am so sorry you had to go through that."

Ella squirmed in my grasp and pulled back. "S'ok, Mama," she murmured. "But..."

"What? What is it?" I asked.

"Why does this keep happening?" Ella whined. "Why do people want to hurt you all the time?"

I closed my eyes at the hurt in her words and her voice. "I-I don't know."

Joseph sat down next to us. "I know why," he said, drawing our attention. "People don't want your mama to stop them from hurting other people. They try to hurt her, and you, because she won't let them hurt others."

Maria looked up at me with tears shining in her eyes. "Y-you save people?"

I nodded.

"Like... like me?" she whispered.

I pulled her closer. "Yes," I whispered back. "Just like with you." I let the girls pull back a little. "I can't let other people suffer just because I might get hurt. I just... can't.

The girls exchanged a glance.

"Would you want me to?" I asked. "If you want me to, I won't try to help people anymore."

"How do you know they need help?" Ella demanded. "How do you know you are stopping bad guys?"

I shrugged. "I don't," I explained. "No one really knows for sure. I just do my best."

"Why do you do it but no one else?"

I sighed. "I have... skills. Abilities. They are like super-powers, in a way." I looked Ella in the eye. "What is it that Spiderman's uncle says?"

Instead of answering, Ella scowled. "Why don't you just give the power back?"

"I can't, honey. No matter how much I want to."

She pulled away, crossing her arms. "I don't like it. I want you to stop."

Maria frowned. "I wish you didn't have to save people, Mama, but I don't think you should stop." She looked at Ella. "Mama is a hero. Heroes are hard to live with, right?" She turned back to me. "If you stopped, you'd be... Wouldn't you be a bad guy?"

"She wouldn't be a bad guy," Ella protested. "She'd be safe. We'd be safe."

"But other people wouldn't," Maria pointed out.

"Girls!" I interrupted their argument. "Look, I know it's hard, and we can talk about this more. I promise, I won't do this again without talking to you first."

Ella crossed her arms. "You won't get poisoned without our permission?"

I smiled. "Good point, kiddo."

Joseph leaned closer. "It is a good point. Sometimes Nicola doesn't get a choice. Because she has the abilities she does, bad guys might try to get her before she even knows about them."

"So," Ella said. "You should stop having the power to help." Her voice sounded doubtful as she said the words.

I frowned. "How do I do that? I mean, I'd be all over that if it was possible...."

Ella dropped her arms. "No, you wouldn't. Grandma says you like the attention."

I blinked in surprise. "Attention? What attention? From who?" I looked around at them surrounding me. "Whose attention would I want aside from the people standing right here? Who would be worth more to me than you?"

The girls shrugged.

I frowned. "Why would grandma say that then? What point is she trying to make? What does she expect me to do?" I sighed. "What is the right thing to do?"

Ella scowled but didn't answer. Maria frowned at her sister, then at me. I sighed and looked at Joseph. He shrugged.

I understood. I didn't have an answer either.

Sarah has been writing for more than 30 years. She lives in the Midwest with two monsters (the kids), an ogre (the hubby), and whatever drama-llama is coming to visit this week. She is the author of the *Runespells* series, and she has short stories in several anthologies, including *Counterclockwise: A Time Travel Anthology*, *Chasing Fireflies*, *Beyond the Mask: A Superhero Anthology Twisted: A Horror Anthology*, and *Visions IV: Between the Stars*. Sarah also runs multiple newsletters, author profiles on several social media platforms, a blog via Patreon, a weekday twitch stream, and makes funny videos about writing on her vlog, *Practically Writing*. As Lina Greyce, she is the author of the *Hot Fae Knights* series.

TOO WYRD
SARAH BUHRMAN

www.ingramcontent.com/pod-product-compliance
Lightning Source LLC
Chambersburg PA
CBHW030855200726
48289CB00003B/762